Recipe for Passion

L. MOONE

CONTENTS

CHAPTER ONE

A man who makes food like this has got to be great in bed.

That's what I've firmly believed ever since I watched Byron Ainsworth's debut on the Home TV Network with his show, *Decadent Desserts*. Only six months into his whirlwind career and he's become a household name who's made it onto many a bored housewife's Celebrity Cheat List. Mine too, if I weren't painfully single.

For this very reason, I was thrilled when the assignment to write an exclusive profile on him landed on my desk. Did I want to spend a whole week at the famous Pinewood Studios on the outskirts of London, shadowing the man who had fueled many a delicious late night fantasy of mine already? Hell yeah! I can't think of a more perfect way to combine some of my favorite things: journalism and beautiful men. Oh, and chocolate of course.

Plus, this could be *the* assignment to get Tom to take me more seriously and start giving me better work at the office. Finally, an exclusive byline just for me. A chance to see my name on the frontpage, even.

He's underlined repeatedly how important this opportunity is, so I can't afford to blow it.

All I have to do is capture the essence of how amazing Byron Ainsworth is in person. How hard can it be?

It's Monday morning when I arrive on set for the very first time. With a spring in my step and a bubbly feeling in my chest, I head out of the visitor parking where I've left my car and right towards the entrance gate of the studio complex to introduce myself.

"Sarah Walker, from *Celeb Roundup*, here to visit the set of *Decadent Desserts*. My office called ahead last week?" I flash my ID and press pass to the guard.

He checks his clipboard and nods. "Right. Go ahead, it's in TV One, just over there."

"Thanks!" Another surge of excitement washes over me as I pass through the open gate and towards the large hangar-like building the guard pointed out. The sun is out, and thanks to the heat wave we've been having, it's uncharacteristically warm for mid-May. I'm taking it as a sign.

Even the weather matches my mood. I smile to myself and try to remember to breathe deeply and slowly.

It's my first time on a TV set, not including a one-time experience as an audience member on a talk show when I was still in college. Although I've never been much of a fan girl of anything, the prospect of meeting Byron Ainsworth is unlike anything I've ever experienced. Despite spending a couple of years at *Celeb Roundup* already, I've only ever had desk assignments. I've never actually met a real life celebrity before, never mind interviewed them. Finally, I get to do the kind of work I've always dreamed about.

A girl who looks to be in her early to mid-twenties stops in her tracks in front of me just as I open the unmarked door.

"Is this the *Decadent Desserts* set?" I ask, showing her my press pass as well.

She nods. "Yep, this is it."

"Great." I don't get the chance to properly introduce myself before she vanishes.

"Claire! The reporter from that gossip website is here." I can hear her voice deeper inside the dimly-lit building. After the bright sunshine outside, it takes my eyes a moment to adjust.

As a table of bottled water and other refreshments comes into view just by the door, that same girl returns, accompanied by someone else—someone a bit more senior looking.

"Hi, I'm Claire. I'm the executive producer here," the bespectacled blonde, perhaps a couple of years older than me, introduces herself while we shake hands. She looks me over, as if to size me up. Yep, she's definitely used to being in charge and comes across as slightly intimidating.

"Sarah Walker, *Celeb Roundup*. Nice to meet you. I guess someone from the office spoke to you already?" I ask.

"Indeed. And you're just in time to meet Byron before we start for the day. Jill, be a dear and check if he's ready." Claire's voice is firm and matter-of-fact. I'm not getting much warmth from her, but then again she's probably just busy and my arrival is yet another thing for her to manage this morning.

I hold my breath and smile through my nerves. "Great!"

Jill, presumably Claire's assistant, flits away again, and I'm left waiting with my heart in my throat. I've been wondering what Byron is like in person… and now I'll find out.

"You can keep your bag over there if you like." Claire points at a row of chairs facing a heightened platform right in the middle of the cavernous building, before vanishing in the buzz of activity all around.

On stage I spot the kitchen cabinets with the signature cottage-style oak wood finish I've seen so many times on the show. So *that's where the magic happens*, as they say.

Crew members are darting back and forth, setting up cameras and adjusting spotlights, but the stage itself is still pretty dark. It's funny how everything looks make-shift and incomplete like this. I imagine that'll change once the lights go on.

"Sarah? Over here." Jill waves at me from the other side of the stage.

I stumble into action and join her by a door with a forbidding yellow 'Private' sticker right in the center.

She knocks twice and peeps inside. "Byron, she's here."

"Come in!" he booms.

What a voice!

Jill gestures at me to go ahead, and I swallow the butterflies in my stomach, pushing the flimsy hardboard door fully open before making my way inside. A part of me wishes she'd accompany me inside, but she doesn't. Into the lion's den I go. And there he is, in front of the lit up mirror, getting his face touched up by a timid looking make-up girl.

"Good morning, Mr. Ainsworth—or, is it okay if I call you Byron?" I ask.

He looks up at the mirror, his reflection revealing a row of blindingly white teeth. They even look a bit fake, especially in this light.

"Byron is fine." He brusquely makes a shooing gesture at the girl to stop what she's doing, prompting her to quickly gather her things and throw them in her bag before leaving us alone. "And your name is?"

I hold my breath while he turns his chair to face me and gets up. He's tall, and a bit lankier than he looks on TV, his face appearing more angular. Is this really the same man? I suppose the make-up makes him appear a bit weird right now, but that's probably necessary or his features would look washed out on camera.

He sticks his hand out in my direction, and I take it.

"Sarah Walker. From *Celeb Roundup.*"

"Right, Sarah. Nice to meet you." His grip is weak and cold, almost creepy. He holds on to my hand a little too long for comfort, which makes the hairs on the back of my neck stand up.

I can't put my finger on what it is exactly, but my spidey senses are tingling. This moment isn't at all how I thought it would be. He doesn't sweep me off my feet with his charismatic personality and winning smile. He doesn't even impress me.

Hate at first sight would be a good way to describe it. A visceral sort of repulsion. The kind of reaction you'd have to the smell of rancid food or the sight of a fat spider lurking in the darkest corner of the shed. The disappointment is immense. As excited as I was only moments ago, now I'm just… deflated.

The small talk that follows feels like pulling teeth. He's trying to play the game—be charming, even compliment me multiple times—but that's only making me retreat more. So, *he's* the Heartthrob Chef? Nuh-uh, I don't think so! I still can't get over how unpleasant he was when he sent that make-up girl away. His arrogance is staggering.

A large part of me wants to bolt right now. Unfortunately, I still have a feature to write. With my room at a nearby Premier Inn booked for until the end of the week, and time cleared in my schedule, it's too late to change my mind. I was desperate to get this job. It was supposed to be easy. I'm learning pretty quickly what major regret feels like.

This is going to be a challenge. I have no idea how I'm going to put a positive spin on my observations for our readers, who are all gagging to get the inside scoop on Home TV's hottest rising star. And Tom was pretty clear when he gave me the job. *Make them fall in love, Sarah! I'll settle for nothing less and neither will the network, or they'll never give us another exclusive.*

To say I'm crushed during this first meeting would be the understatement of the century. Until the door creaks behind me, and someone else walks in, rescuing me from the unpleasantness of being alone with Byron.

"What the hell, Ethan? Where have you been?" Byron asks. "We're about to start!"

I turn my head and am awestruck by the man who's currently blocking the door. At well over six feet tall, and with broad shoulders to match, he's almost bigger than the doorframe he just entered through. I wouldn't really call him muscular, though. He's more of a cuddly giant rather than a scary one, and yet I'm absolutely lost for words. My heart is racing and my eyes are glued to his. Blue with a hint of green; full, sensual lips and an even fuller head of dark blonde hair. *This.* This is what I'd hoped to feel during my first encounter with Byron. This is the sort of thing Tom wants me to write about.

The butterflies. The odd lump in my throat. The floaty feeling in my chest. How ironic. The feelings are completely right, but they're for the wrong guy.

He seems equally flustered by my presence. Or maybe he's just stunned by my mute psycho stare.

"This is Sarah, the reporter. Remember what I told you the other day, yeah?" Byron says. "Sarah, meet my sous-chef, Ethan."

Byron's tone when he addresses Ethan rubs me the wrong way. But it doesn't seem to bother the gentle giant in front of me, who pays Byron no mind as he offers me his hand.

"Welcome, Sarah. While you're here, if there's anything you need at all... Just let me know and it'll be done," he says.

That voice. That is the voice Byron should have had. And the firm handshake Byron should have offered me, rather than the weak-ass way he just held my hand for too long.

"Thanks so much. Sorry, what did you say your name was?"

"Ethan," he says with a brief smile.

RECIPE FOR PASSION

Oh God. I'm done for.

Before I get to swoon any longer, Jill returns to get everything back on schedule. She leads me to a chair near one of the camera monitors where Claire is already sitting with a headset on and I follow on autopilot. Claire nods a brief acknowledgement in my direction, which finally makes me snap out of my trance.

What the hell just happened?

My heart rate takes a good while to settle down to something close to normal; meanwhile the lights come on and everyone gets into position to start recording.

I let my eyes wander across the darkened studio and the various members of the production team as I calm down. I do a double take when I spot Jill talking to one of the camera guys who vaguely reminds me of Ethan, only not quite. The man himself isn't anywhere within sight. I wonder what he does here the whole day? There's never been anyone else on the show except Byron. Why would a TV chef need a sous-chef anyway? Doesn't he just prepare all the food live in front of the cameras?

"Quiet, everyone! Let's roll!" Claire calls out next to me before leaning forward to check the feed from the various camera angles on her tablet.

I sigh and shake my head at myself. Remembering Claire's last instruction, I grab my phone out of my bag and put it on silent.

That's when I see a message waiting from my bestie from work, Megan, who writes the regular lifestyle column.

'How goes?'

I can't help but take the bait and send her a barrage of messages. About Byron. About his fake looking teeth and arrogant demeanor. All of it. Except for the moment of relief I felt once Ethan arrived in the changing room.

'I thought this feature was my golden ticket, ya know? And a chance to meet TV's most eligible bachelor. But he's horrible! Everything you think he is from watching the show, right? He's the exact opposite,' I write.

'Ha! You can't put any of that into your article, darling. Tom will kill you.'

I hate that she's right.

I sink deeper into my chair and shoot a sullen glance in Byron's direction. I wish I could just write about Ethan instead. The feature would practically write itself.

'I know,' I write back.

It takes Meg a couple of seconds to send her reply. 'It's supposed to be a fluff piece. Think of the readers. Think of the advertising revenue. He's everyone's favorite of the month. Nobody wants to read about his creepy, clammy hands.'

I roll my eyes. She sounds exactly like Tom, and I don't want to hear it.

'It's the truth, though,' I respond.

Should I tell her about Ethan now? Probably. Maybe. But that'll require a lot more time than what I can get away with. Beside me, Claire is still completely focused on the camera feeds, but she's bound to notice my absentmindedness sooner or later. She already seemed annoyed by my presence here, so I should do my best to blend in.

Meanwhile, Megan is still typing. 'Tough shit. Nobody visits celeb gossip sites for the boring old truth. They want glamour! They want to imagine themselves bent over that floury kitchen counter while he impales them with his... rolling pin.'

That would have been funny, if the mental image wasn't also so off-putting. And she does have a point. I guess this is where the reality of being a tabloid journalist doesn't match the dream. I don't happen to like the subject of my feature, but the readers do. Plus, Tom made a deal with the network. Ugh. I suppose it's still miles better than the opposite scenario: having to tear someone down whom I do like as a person.

I make a face at my phone and stuff it back into my bag, then I open up my notepad and try to figure out what's going on beyond the stage lighting. I've never been to a cooking show shoot before, but it still surprises me how many tries Byron-effing-Ainsworth needs to whip up a basic meringue. Again, these candid observations are not too useful for my article, but I scribble them down anyway.

I start wondering how I'm going to survive a whole week of this when Ethan walks onto the set, carrying several bowls of ingredients, probably. I peer across at Claire's screen to get a closer look.

Ethan is delicious. Despite the few extra pounds he's carrying around the waist, or perhaps even because of them? Here's a man who seems to have a real appetite for life, unlike Byron, who just looks miserable all around. Someone to cuddle with on the sofa while sharing a pint of choco-chip ice cream. A *real* man, not a cardboard cut-out of one with fake bleached teeth, plucked eyebrows, and a clammy, weak handshake.

The stage—Byron and all—fades into the background until I barely even realize it's still there. All I have eyes for is Ethan. My pen is moving across the page with a mind of its own, recording any and all impressions I have of him. How watching him interact with Byron makes me feel. How I wish *he* were the star of the show instead.

I wonder how old he is? Mid-thirties, maybe? Definitely a few years older than me, but not outrageously so...

Okay, I *can* do this for a week. I'll just

interview *him* most of the time. I'll call it background research, or something. Learn about the inner workings of the show from him and brainstorm a new angle for my piece at the same time.

Yes, that could work. Ethan did tell me he'd make sure I get *anything I need.* It's probably a good thing he doesn't know where my mind went as soon as he said that.

CHAPTER TWO

*** Ethan ***

Her name is Sarah.

She turned my world upside-down the moment I came across her in Byron's dressing room.

I already know she's going to be the last thing on my mind as I go to sleep tonight, and the first thing I'll think about tomorrow morning. Such is the impact she's had on me during those few minutes of our first meeting.

Byron—being Byron—had pawned her off on me the second he found out a reporter was coming at all. *Whatever she needs, whenever she needs it; take care of it.* Those were his exact words. *And don't fuck up! We need to make a good impression or it'll be both our jobs.*

At the time, I'd wanted to protest and tell him how precious my time was. That I should spend it focusing on my own work; that he'd be nowhere right now if it wasn't for me doing what I do. That Jill should be handling the reporter. As Claire's assistant, this sort of thing is one of her responsibilities anyway. Of course, I didn't *say* any of that. Because I know better than anyone how Byron gets when people refuse his demands.

But then I saw Sarah in person and forgot all about how busy my schedule already was. My objections melted away like butter underneath the bright spotlights.

She'd smiled and introduced herself and I was instantly enamored by her. I could barely get a coherent greeting out while she shook my hand. Those slender fingers. So fragile and soft in my much larger paw-like hand. The rest of her, as well. Gentle hazel eyes, auburn hair, a few freckles adorning the tip of her nose. And a figure to die for, with curves in all the right places. Everything about her is perfect and completely unlike me.

She took my breath away and I knew instantly I'll never meet another woman like her.

Her presence had me reeling even now with emotions I couldn't quite identify or know how to handle. It changed me. Within a split second I became infused with an obsession so deep, I know there's no chance of ignoring it. Like when you add vanilla extract to literally anything. Hard as you may try to cover it up, it'll always be there in the background. Spending any amount of time with her will lead me into even more dangerous territory, and yet…

"Anything you need at all. Just let me know and it'll be done," I'd told her. I meant it. *Anything.*

She'd smiled brightly, which inspired an unfamiliar

warm feeling in my chest. "Thanks so much. Sorry, what did you say your name was?"

Even her voice is angelic.

I'd mumbled my answer while trying hard not to stare.

Jill interrupted that little moment to get Sarah settled in to watch the shoot, allowing me the chance to breathe again. That was only an hour ago, and yet it feels like she's the woman I've been waiting for my entire life. Ridiculous. I don't even know the first thing about her.

Anyway, it was time to set up the ingredients for the first shot, so I quickly ducked out of there and into my own private refuge: the backstage prep kitchen. And that's where I've been ever since. Just how in the hell am I supposed to concentrate on my work when I know she's still out there?

And she'll continue to be out there for the rest of the damn week. Observing. Taking notes. Interviewing people. Taking pictures. And all the while, being utterly perfect. Way too perfect for the likes of me. I've never thought of myself as a hopeless romantic, but she's converted me with a smile.

"Ethan, fucking get in here!" I hear Byron's muffled bark through the closed door.

Here we go again. It's the same thing during every shoot.

"Yeah, what's the problem?" I respond, while

training my eyes on the stage area. *Don't try to look for her! Don't get side-tracked!*

It's going to be a long and hard day. But the thought of interacting with her again makes it easier for me to keep going.

*** Sarah ***

Thank the stars, the shoot is over. Save for Byron's meltdown when his meringue kept collapsing, the day was dull and uneventful. I never imagined how boring a cooking show set would be. The same steps, recorded over and over and over again. I guess I expected it all to be done in real-time with the camera only playing the role of silent observer.

Worse still, I only got to see Ethan briefly; he was mostly off-set after our initial meeting, except for when he was carrying bowls of food back and forth.

Even after the lights go off, there's still no sign of him. I wander around the studio and talk to anyone and everyone who can spare a moment. They all say the same kind of stuff.

Byron Ainsworth is a saint of a man and a joy to work with.

I feel privileged to be a part of such a successful show.

The food is as amazing as it looks.

Everyone has gained a few pounds, just tasting stuff that

he's made while shooting.

Yada yada. I stop taking notes after the third person gives me the exact same spiel. It all sounds a little too similar. A little too flawless, not unlike Byron's teeth.

But then Jill fixes me a plate of samplers from the day's episode, and I have to admit that they weren't wrong about that part. The food *is* amazing. A little too amazing. It's difficult not to over-indulge. If I was surrounded by this stuff every day, I'd gain a bunch of weight too.

Any man who makes food like this has got to be great in bed.

This was going to be my angle, of sorts, for the article. I was going to play on how sexy it is when a man cooks for you. Byron's expert use of aphrodisiac ingredients. And how handsome and charismatic he is in person. My concept was going to be something along the lines of " *A Dinner Date with Byron Ainsworth, the Heartthrob Chef.* " Exactly the sort of positive buzz Tom had asked for.

Thinking back to all these ideas I'd brainstormed in the safety of my desk at the office makes me throw up in my mouth a little.

If I'm going to survive this week with my self-worth and credibility intact, I will need to put a new spin on things. I quickly clean the last remnants of whipped cream off my plate and check my notes again. Every time I see Ethan's name mentioned, I can't stop myself from smiling. For now, I'll indulge the urge to follow up on him instead.

"Umm, Claire?" I call out. "Sorry to disturb you."

It occurs to me that she's the only person Byron didn't get snippy with even once today. Not sure if it's an on-set hierarchy thing, or just the take-no-shit attitude she projects. She *is* rather intimidating, after all.

"Not at all. Are you getting everything you need?" she asks. "I can schedule some time for your first sit-down with Byron tonight, if you like."

I shake my head, thinking of an excuse to delay being alone with him. "I'll take some time to get used to being on set first," I tell her. "Actually, what's in there?" I point at the door through which I'd seen Ethan disappear earlier.

"Oh, that's just the prep area. A lot of the food can't take the heat of the lights, so we only bring things out at the last minute. It's pretty standard for shows like this." Claire smiles and nods as if to emphasize her own statement.

"Okay, so—what's-his-name—Ethan is in charge of that, is he?" I ask, nonchalantly pretending to take notes. The last thing I want is to appear overly keen.

"Right. He's Byron's sous-chef. He helps out, you know. Behind the scenes." She clears her throat, but doesn't say anything else.

"And they've been working together for a while, yes?"

"Sure. They've come up in the restaurant business together. Known each other for years." Claire waves at the girl who first greeted me when I got here. "Jill, can you get Sarah here a cup of coffee, or—how do you take your coffee? Or would you prefer something else?"

"Tea with milk, no sugar. Thanks." I smile at Jill, who rushes away again, then turn my attention back to Claire, who looks like she's pretty much done with our conversation.

"Okay, so I don't want to bother Mr. Ainsworth unnecessarily as I'm sure he's very busy. Maybe I can get time with Ethan first in order to get some history?"

Claire frowns briefly. "Okay, if that's what you want."

"It is indeed."

"I'll make it happen."

"Thank you *so* much." I walk back to my seat with a frisson of excitement building in my chest. Step one of my mission: accomplished. Now, I'd better get some questions down on the page. I wouldn't want to end up face-to-face with the new man of my dreams without anything to say.

I'm halfway through my list of discussion points for Ethan when my phone starts buzzing in my bag.

"Oh, hi Tom." I try to sound upbeat.

"Sarah. Just checking in."

I suppress a sigh. He's never ever *just* checking in.

"Yeah, I've been on set all day. It's interesting."

"Great stuff. Say, how would you feel about getting some exclusive video? Marketing is telling me that Byron is trending on YouTube at the moment. I'd like to cash in on that and create buzz for our feature."

I pinch the bridge of my nose. "Sure, Tom. I'll get it done."

"ASAP, alright Sarah? I need something by tomorrow. And I need top quality work on this assignment, okay? This is your shot, don't waste it. No pressure."

"Done."

I wince and stuff the phone into my pocket. What have I gotten myself into? I've trashed my original concept for the story, and the alternative is nebulous at best. Oh, who am I kidding? I've got *nothing!*

Tom has been very clear from the start what I'm here for. This is a favor, which goes both ways. Byron normally doesn't talk to the press, but Tom's insider at the network made it happen anyway.

Despite being online-only, *Celeb Roundup* is first to get exclusive access to Byron. In exchange, we're meant to build excitement and hype for the upcoming season of *Decadent Desserts*. It's supposed to be a win-

win for both parties.

And I flat-out begged for this assignment, because I'd enjoyed the last season of the show. And because I have a huge sweet tooth. It sounded like the perfect opportunity, and it's turning out to be anything but.

If I want to make it in this job, I can't let Tom down. But I can't stomach the idea of lying outright either. I might just be a budding tabloid journalist, but I do have *some* principles and standards. My credibility is important to me, and singing Byron's praises goes against everything my intuition is trying to tell me. I've got a choice to make, and quickly.

CHAPTER THREE

* Ethan *

The day went by surprisingly smoothly. Only the one temper tantrum? That has to be a new record. Byron has been on his best behavior to make a good impression on Sarah, and as a result I've enjoyed the peace and quiet of my sanctuary far away from the spotlights. I'm grateful this place is so closed off, because any time I've found myself even in the same general space as Sarah, I could only think of one thing: how to make her mine. As if she'd ever be interested in a guy like me.

An unexpected interruption comes along in the form of a knock on the door. Claire's head appears through the crack.

"Ethan. That reporter wants to talk to you today. Are you free?"

Shit .

"Uh, talk to *me?* Why? Isn't she here to interview Byron?" I stammer.

"It'll give her background or whatever. Anyway, shall I tell her four?"

No way! "Okay."

"Great." Claire scrutinizes me for a moment. "You're definitely okay with that, yeah? Just stick to the basics. We'll get drinks after to discuss strategy for the coming week."

"Don't worry, it'll be absolutely fine. I'll take care of her."

Claire gives me a thumbs up and shuts the door behind her. My assurances might have been enough to satisfy her, but I'm reeling inside. What the hell just happened? Why didn't I refuse like I should have done? It's all on Claire and her infuriating ability to get everyone—Byron included—to do exactly what she wants, when she wants it. A talent I wish I possessed, especially if I'm going to spend time alone with Sarah today.

Which leads me to the most important consideration of all right now: what's the time?

A glance at my watch sends me into a fresh panic. I only have about fifteen minutes to get my head on straight.

Deep breaths.

It's going to be fine, I tell myself. *All you've got to do is answer some questions about Byron. No big deal.*

OK, that last part isn't right. It feels like a huge deal. Because of course I want nothing more than to spend time with Sarah, especially if it's just the two of us. Get to know her. Figure out if we click somehow. But that's not what she's here for. We each have a role to play and we're definitely *not* on the same side!

I take a look around the prep area. What a mess! Pots and pans, bowls and whisks; everything is strewn about as though a tornado has passed through here. That's kind of my style in the kitchen. I can be chaotic when I'm in the zone, but I like to think that the end result more than makes up for it. I try to make a start on the giant clean-up operation in front of me, when there's yet another knock on the door.

"Just a moment, Claire!" I call out, vigorously scraping blobs of dried up pastry dough off the steel countertop.

"Oh, I'm sorry. You're looking for Claire? Shall I get her for you?" Sarah's soft voice behind me all but makes my heart stop. I drop the scraper onto the table and slowly turn around.

"Shit. I thought you were—" I start. "Hi, Sarah. Claire told me you were coming." At four! She said you were coming at freaking four, not right now!

I wipe my hands dry on a clean dish towel and shoot a reluctant glance in her direction. Damn, she's breathtaking. How on earth am I supposed to play it cool?

"If you're busy, I can come back later?" Her brown eyes are wide and there's the subtlest hint of a smile playing on her lips.

"No, that won't help," I blurt out.

"What?"

"I mean, now is fine." Get a grip, man! "Take a seat; make yourself comfortable. I'll be right there."

She turns towards the random grouping of chairs and stools beside the door. Leftover props the studio has found fit to dump in here. For a change, they serve a purpose rather than just being in my way.

Sarah sits down, right next to the chair that holds my unceremoniously dumped backpack and crumpled up jacket. I try desperately to be cool as I watch her open her notepad and click the top of her ballpoint pen. Maybe it was for the best that I didn't get all that time to prepare. The anticipation of spending any amount of time alone with her only turned me into more of a wreck.

"Really. If I'm disturbing you, just say so," she says, smiling sweetly at me.

As if! She could ask me for the world and saying 'no' wouldn't even be an option. Instead she's only hoping for a conversation. Such a small thing.

"Not at all. What would you like to know?" I reply, folding my arms and leaning against the counter opposite her. Realizing how tiny she looks sitting down in front of me, and how I must be looming over her like a complete freak, I unfold my arms again and grab a stool for myself as well.

Sarah mindlessly chews on the end of her pen for a moment, before tapping on the paper and looking up at me again. "There's a lot to get through, but what I'm most curious about is this. How—in your own words—did all of this come about? The show. Your working relationship with Byron. All of it? From the beginning, please."

That's an awfully vague question. As if she's hoping I'll trip up somewhere.

"I've known Byron for years, actually," I start. Although I should probably keep things short, there's something in Sarah's eyes that makes me want to elaborate, while sticking as close to the truth as possible. "Worked a few odd jobs side by side, trained under Jack Cleary at his Kingston restaurant…"

"Oh, the Michelin star chef?" Sarah furiously scribbles down her notes. I try to ignore how impressed she sounds. This isn't about me and my ego.

I clear my throat. "Yeah, the one. He was discovered there, actually. It was completely random, a suit from the network had come in for lunch and was so impressed by a particular dish he ordered that he wanted to speak to the chef who'd invented it… So, when they decided to give Byron his own show, he brought me onboard as well." And there we go. I've placed myself back in the backseat where I belong, with Byron at the wheel.

"Old friends, then?" She nods encouragingly while finishing another sentence on the page.

"Sure. Old friends." And that's where the bullshit

really begins. I try to ignore the little twinge in my chest. A little white lie never hurt anyone, right? Especially not when told to someone who could unravel your entire career with the stroke of a pen.

"So what happens here, exactly?" She gestures at the messy and disorganized kitchen setup with the back of her pen. "Claire said you have to keep some ingredients away from the heat of the spotlights for as long as possible, hence the need for a completely separate area. Forgive me if these are dumb questions. But I've never been to a cooking show shoot before, and neither have most of my readers."

I follow her line of sight towards the staggering array of mixing bowls, saucepans, and other cooking paraphernalia I've used today. "Right, yes. Things like butter, whipped cream, and chocolate tend to melt very easily. Umm…"

"You do the prep work single-handedly?" she interjects. "And you make sure the dishes look good for the camera?"

"Yes to both. Prep and plating. Basically it's exactly the same as what a sous chef would do in a restaurant kitchen. Byron calls the shots, and I try to help out where I can."

That's the story, and I'm sticking to it.

Sarah remains silent for a moment, so the only sound between us is the gentle scratch of her writing her notes. She's adorable, sitting there with her hair tied up in a loose bun and delicate fingers wrapped around the pen she's holding. We've had an early heat wave this year, so she's wearing an airy short sleeved blouse on top of her well fitted jeans. She's a beautiful woman, despite the clothes she seems to have chosen more for comfort than anything else, or perhaps because of them. Because there's nothing pretentious about her. She's not even wearing any make-up as far as I can tell. Nor any visible jewelry.

She's the exact opposite of all the fans who tend to visit Byron's meet and greet events.

As she puts a period behind the final word on the page, I see a little quiver in her. It seems to start from in between her shoulder blades and passes through her entire body. A subtle wave of goose bumps travels down her bare arms and she looks even smaller and more fragile than before.

She doesn't complain, but I can't ignore what I saw. Even her lips appear to have turned a few shades, making them appear almost purple. Perhaps I'm only imagining that part.

"You're cold," I observe.

She looks up at me and shrugs. "It's okay."

It's not, though. I can't stand it. Whereas she's mostly made me nervous so far, I feel something else now. An unfamiliar urgency, a protective instinct of sorts.

"We can continue the interview someplace else.

Someplace warmer," I suggest. Perhaps go for a walk on the grounds outside, or…

Sarah smiles and shakes her head. "Really, it's fine. A little chill has never killed anyone."

I get up from my seat and pick up my jacket from the chair beside her. A waft of her subtle perfume hits me, and jumbles my thoughts.

"At least take this," I tell her.

She accepts my offering and stares at me for a moment with those big hazel eyes of hers. Yet she doesn't say anything.

This is a creepy move, isn't it? Who the hell would accept some stranger's clothes? Jeez, all I was supposed to do was answer a few questions, and now my oafish attempt at being helpful is making me come across like a pervert. *Good job!*

"Or better yet—" I quickly take a step back and gesture at the stove behind me. "I'll make us something warm to drink."

She lays the folded garment carefully across her lap and smiles briefly. "Thanks, that would be lovely, actually. Claire had asked that girl, Jill, to get me a cup of tea, but she must have forgotten about it."

"Jill is great, but frankly she's too busy to keep up with everything," I remark, while picking up the only clean saucepan left on the counter and gathering some essential ingredients. "It won't take five minutes; hang in there."

RECIPE FOR PASSION

* Sarah *

Holy hell. When he got up and leaned over me to reach for his jacket, I was sure I was going to faint. It was in equal parts a relief as well as a crushing disappointment when he backed away from me a split second later. My heart is thumping so loudly, I'm convinced he can hear it too.

Great effort being professional, you idiot!

Still, watching Ethan get to work in the kitchen is a sight for sore eyes. He's a large man, and yet he moves back and forth between the huge double door fridge and the stove with grace and confidence I couldn't muster if I tried. He's everything Byron isn't, in person.

Although I am chilled to the bone, and want nothing more than to take that jacket of his and engulf myself in it, I resist. Being surrounded by something of his—especially something as well-worn as this slightly faded khaki summer jacket—would overwhelm me and turn me into a puddle of mush. My pride won't allow it, not with him watching over me. I'm a reporter, dammit! Not a damsel in distress.

His scent, though! I caught a whiff of it when we first met, and am still getting little hints of it from the garment I'm white-knuckling in my lap. Manly, yet sweet. A pinch of musk and the promise of exotic spices. Or is that the treat he's cooking up on the stove?

Either way, I'm done for. My heart is racing, and I've pretty much forgotten what I was going to ask him next. How the hell am I supposed to get through this interview without making a fool of myself?

Would it be absolutely terrible of me to try to flirt with him? He probably isn't interested, but how would I know, unless I gave it a shot?

Megan would have a field day with me if I told her any of this. I should call her the second I get back to my hotel, because I desperately need to vent. Or gush. Whatever. Anything, just to figure out what I'm doing with this damn feature before Tom gets on my case about it. He's bound to start asking about my concept as soon as I send him the video footage he asked for.

And right now, I've got absolutely nothing.

By the time Ethan pours the contents of his saucepan into a large stoneware mug, I feel all warm and fuzzy inside just from being able to stare at him in peace. He was too busy to notice, and had his back turned for much of it, so I try not to feel too guilty.

This is what I was hoping for when I asked Tom for the assignment. It sounded like a trip to heaven. A whole week of watching Byron Ainsworth cook up a storm for the cameras, only to get him all to myself after hours. For interviewing purposes, obviously.

I had no way of knowing that I'd have this very

same reaction to someone I didn't even know existed until this morning. Someone who is so unlike Byron in every possible way, that I can hardly believe they get along at all. And yet, they're supposed to be old friends…

On top of that, he's not even my type, in the traditional sense, and yet I'm swooning like a teenager.

Ethan finally presents me with a steaming hot mug, which I gratefully accept. Our fingers brush against each other, making me shiver even more intensely than before. How is he so warm?

I try to ignore that thought and focus on the treat he's cooked up. The sweet, seductive aromas tickle my senses until I can no longer resist. If I wasn't already so smitten, the very first sip would have converted me for sure.

Screw Byron. Ethan is a god among men.

"Oh fuck, this is really good!" I blurt out.

He suppresses a chuckle. "Don't sound so surprised. I am a chef, remember?"

I crinkle my nose and give him an apologetic smirk. "Yeah, that's fair enough."

Another little sip of the rich chocolaty concoction, and I can't stop grinning. "It's just that hot chocolate is my favorite thing in the whole world. And this has got to be the best one I've ever tasted."

He sinks back down onto his stool again, cocks his

head to the side, and just observes me. "I'm glad you like it. Hope it helps you warm up."

That it does. As does the way he's looking at me. Could it be that he might be interested in me too, just a little bit? My mind starts conjuring up other ways in which he could heat me up, when I force myself back on track.

He's probably just enjoying the compliment, I conclude. Nothing in our interactions so far has indicated that he's considering our conversation as anything other than a work obligation. I've still got a few days to figure it out, though. And an equal number of lonely nights in that hotel room to spend fantasizing about what might be.

Ethan folds his arms and I swallow the urge to imagine what they'd feel like if he wrapped them around me instead.

Focus, woman!

"What else did you want to know?" he asks, his expression serious and business-like again.

"Everything," I whisper.

"Sorry?"

"I mean there are still quite a few questions left," I mumble, forcing my gaze down onto my notepad.

"Okay, well, I'll do my best to give you anything you need."

I almost choke on the remainder of the hot chocolate while I imagine just how this scenario would play out if this were all a dream…

CHAPTER FOUR

*** Ethan ***

The interview is over, and Sarah has left the building. Well, at least she's left my kitchen, for now.

I'm utterly confused. Did that go well? Did I manage to give her the answers she wanted, without giving too much of myself away? When I finally get around to cleaning my workspace like I'd wanted to do before the interview, I can't stop myself from replaying every interaction of ours in my head a thousand times.

I'm definitely obsessed.

Even when I close my eyes for a moment, I can still see her. The dreamy expression in her eyes when she tasted the hot chocolate I'd whipped up was the highlight of not just my day, but my year so far.

She was beaming. I would give anything to get her to smile at me like that again. And again.

This is why I got into the food industry in the first place. To make people happy in a way only a good meal can achieve. It's the only reason I agreed to leave my job at Jack Cleary's restaurant with Byron. The payoff for having to actually deal with him and his constant bullshit on a daily basis made it seem worth it at the time, because I knew these recipes would be enjoyed by a much wider audience than I could hope to reach on my own.

Still, making something—even if it's only a very basic hot chocolate with a spicy twist—and actually getting the credit for it is an entirely new feeling. One I could get used to.

Or maybe that's just because it was for Sarah. I'd love to cook something else for her one of these days. Maybe the next time she wants to talk to me.

If there is a next time.

I pause and put the scrubber down into the sink. What if that's the solution?

While I'm not much to look at—not remotely photogenic like Byron, anyway—what if this is one way I could get through to her? Who doesn't like good food, right? If the way to a man's heart is supposedly through his stomach, why couldn't the same approach work here? Sarah might be gorgeous and out of my league in every possible way, but she really seems to have a sweet tooth. I may not be a player; I don't even know the damn *game*. But I know my way around a kitchen…

It's a better plan than nothing at all. Something to aim for. I like to think I'm nice enough, once someone takes the time to get to know me. Reliable and trustworthy, even. I would spend a lifetime toiling to make up for every one of my shortcomings, if only it meant I could spend it with her.

I may not be the star of the show, but perhaps that's not a deal breaker. I'm sure she's interviewed enough celebrities as part of her job that that sort of thing wouldn't even impress her much anymore. Maybe. Hopefully.

Once I'm done tidying up, I pick up my things and look for Claire. I find her as well as Jill and the others in the editing room, deciding between takes from today's raw footage.

She rolls back in her chair when she spots me. "Ethan! How did it go with Sarah?"

"Good, I think," I say.

She nods and checks the screen again while shaking her head. "Not this one; Byron looks like he's about to throw the bowl at the camera. Try the next take."

"Okay, so what can I do for you?" She turns to me again and adjusts the glasses on her nose. "We're not running low on any ingredients, are we?"

I shake my head. "No, we're all set. I've just been thinking about how to manage things this week. With Sarah."

Claire gestures at Jill to hand her the iPad.

"Byron has a fan meet and greet before we start rolling in the morning, so I'm going to suggest she sits in on that," Claire says. "Other than that… She hasn't been asking any awkward questions, has she?"

"Not at all." Not yet, anyway. "We basically talked about Byron and our previous job together."

"Good. I wouldn't want her to get in the way of anything. I'm going to have to think of a few ways to keep her busy during most of her time here. Ideally the network should have never allowed this, but what can you do? Someone higher up insisted. I don't have the clout to refuse."

My heart skips a beat. Great. So Claire wants to keep her distracted. That means keeping her away from Byron and the shoots.

"I could prepare a tasting menu of highlights from the previous season, as well as some previews of upcoming episodes?" I wonder. "That'll keep her busy for a while."

"Excellent idea. The more she focuses on the food, the better," Claire says. "That's what the show is about, anyway. The rest is just window-dressing."

That's something we can both agree on. And it gives me an excellent excuse to spend more time alone with her. It's the perfect solution to all our problems.

"Okay, done. You can suggest it to her next time you see her." I smile. "We're still on for drinks later? Jill?"

Jill gives me the thumbs up from across the room, then puts her headphones back on.

"We'll be done here within the hour. See you down at the pub." Claire has already turned away again and is fully focused on the screen in front of her.

Excellent. My plan is shaping up.

I might not be confident in my abilities to chat up and charm members of the opposite sex, but when it comes to cooking, I know I've got what it takes to impress. Let's hope Sarah feels the same way.

*** Sarah ***

Day two at the studio starts 'in media res' as they say in the movie business. I'm thrown right in the middle of the action as a horde of excited fans of the show arrive at a nearby hotel for their exclusive meet and greet with Byron.

I want to pull them aside one by one and tell them to simmer down and not expect too much. That everything they're feeling right now is just misplaced media hype and mob hysteria. But of course I do nothing of the sort. I stand back with my DSLR and observe as the throng of women in their thirties, forties, and even fifties showers Byron with the sort of attention usually reserved for rock stars and A-list actors.

He *is* the Heartthrob Chef after all. Even if I can't

see it anymore.

Maybe that makes *me* the odd one out. I still can't shake the creeping sense of disgust as I record him, confidently shaking hands, exchanging hugs and posing for selfies all while handing out stacks of signed photos. He's obviously in his element. As is everyone else.

It was this arrogance I didn't like about him yesterday. A sense of entitlement, like he's worthy of all this fuss and fanfare and other people only exist to stroke his over-inflated ego.

For my money, he isn't worth shit. Again. I can't write that, can I? Hopefully I'm at least capturing the sort of footage Tom needs for his YouTube teaser…

Once I'm done recording almost half an hour of candid video, I start to take notes. I observe and analyze all the goings on before me, almost like a *real* reporter, rather than a mouthpiece with a specific mission. With a bit of effort, I'm able to keep my notes objective and devoid of four-letter curses, but to put an entirely positive spin on everything is still too much to ask.

When the fans are finally taken on their guided tour of the set, I find myself alone with Byron, who thankfully has remained sans make-up this morning. At least he looks like a person today and not a caricature of himself. He smiles one of his big bright smiles at me, which I try to reciprocate.

"It's crazy, isn't it?" he remarks. "Seven months ago, nobody even knew my name."

"That's so true." I quickly scribble his remark onto my notepad. Finally, a quote I can use which doesn't make either of us look bad. I wish I'd got this bit on camera.

"We have a little while before I have to be on set, so how about that interview?" he suggests.

"Yes, that would be great." I take a deep breath and flip a page back to a list of questions I'd prepared back at the office. "Let's start at the beginning, shall we?"

It doesn't take much prompting from my side to get Byron going. The man sure can talk, even if there isn't much substance in his words. When I realize there's no hope of even my fastest scribbles keeping up with him, I turn on my voice recorder instead. And once I do that, it doesn't take long before my thoughts wander towards Ethan again.

What a man.

I'd wanted to get Meg's perspective on him yesterday evening, but she never answered my call. So all I did for most of the night was toss and turn and think of the way he handed me his jacket once he saw me shiver. That was a sign, wasn't it? You don't just offer your clothes to a girl unless there's some attraction there.

Unless he's just genuinely a nice guy.

I still regret not wearing it, just in case I never get a chance like that again.

The clock is ticking and before I know it, it'll be time to go home. If only I can come up with a good excuse to spend time alone with Ethan in his kitchen again… I'll bring it up with Claire next time I see her.

Maybe I'll talk to Ethan about the actual dishes; that would be a good excuse, wouldn't it?

Hell, I could focus my feature entirely on the food instead of the man himself like I'd planned to before. *That's it!* I won't have to betray my instincts and will still deliver on Tom's demand for positive coverage of the show.

Re-energized, I scribble that last thought down in my notepad while Byron is still talking up a storm into my voice recorder.

Focus on the food!

Relief washes over me and I find myself smiling as I carry on pretending to listen to Byron's ramblings. Once he leaves for his shoot, I'll find a quiet corner for myself to start putting the pieces of my plan together. And edit that footage Tom wanted as well.

And maybe I'll talk to Claire about getting more time with Ethan to talk about the food itself. Yes, that could work.

CHAPTER FIVE

*** Ethan ***

Evening can't come soon enough. Although it's a relatively short day of shooting because of the fan event this morning, the hours still seem to drag on. It doesn't help that the whole crew stayed out just a little bit too late last night. Especially me and Claire, who lingered on even when most of the juniors went home.

It's a weird bubble to live in: all of us, stuck in this studio for weeks on end. Due to the NDAs we've all signed, nobody is allowed to talk to outsiders about what happens on set, so we really only have each other to share with. Friendships with colleagues become inevitable.

It's a very similar atmosphere to a restaurant kitchen, actually.

It's always the most stressful of work environments that create the strongest bonds simply through the shared experience. There's a certain camaraderie you just wouldn't find in most other jobs.

And so, a few rounds into the night, I finally spilled my guts to Claire. I told her how I felt the moment I first laid eyes on Sarah that morning. And how my attraction only deepened when she came to interview me after the shoot. How I have no clue what to do about it, but I know I can't just ignore it either.

She nodded knowingly as she nursed the third pint on the bar counter in front of her. As if she wasn't even surprised. That's the thing about Claire. She's got the best poker face I've ever seen on a person.

Unfortunately she didn't have much in the way of wisdom to share. In her own words, she's been too damn busy with her career to think of having a love life of her own, so I shouldn't look to her for actionable advice. Fair enough. But at least she provided a sympathetic ear for my rambling thoughts.

Luckily, my admission didn't change her mind about having me cook up a tasting menu for Sarah today. Realistically, this is still the most viable way to keep her out of everyone's hair.

And my best shot at getting what *I* want as well.

Thankfully today's dishes are rather easy, and Byron manages on his own for most of the afternoon. It's about damn time too. If only he'd spend a little less time playing star to his fans and a little more time practicing the recipes, we wouldn't waste so much time shooting each episode.

Instead of fighting fires on stage, I can focus on getting that tasting menu planned out and prepared.

All the favorites from the previous season are represented, as well as a few new dishes. As time approaches, everything is mostly done, except for one which I'll have to prepare on the spot.

I make it a point to have a saucepan of hot chocolate ready and waiting on the stove for when Sarah gets here. Now that I've got a game plan for our interactions, I'm less of a nervous wreck. Instead, I'm filled with a steely determination to impress her by any means necessary.

It's 6:30 sharp when a knock on the door signals her arrival.

"Hi, Ethan, hope I'm not disturbing anything?" Sarah asks as she opens the door.

"Never." I clear my throat. Not a nervous wreck, my ass. "I mean, Claire told me you'd be coming." Hell, it was my own idea to do this in the first place!

"Great. She hinted that there'd be something special waiting for me." She pauses halfway between the door and the row of chairs and stares at the stove. "No way, you've already made hot chocolate?"

The way she looks up and grins at me absolutely kills me.

"Ah, that's only the beginning. I hope you're hungry, because I've prepared samples of all of last season's highlights as well as some new dishes from upcoming episodes," I say. I've also switched off the AC, so she won't feel cold. But I keep that bit to myself.

Her eyes widen. "I'm famished. I skipped lunch today."

"Good."

"You'll have to talk me through it all, okay?"

"Sure." I smile.

"Do you mind if I record this? It's more efficient than taking notes in the moment."

"Whatever you need," I say.

She opens her bag and takes out a digital camera and a foldable tripod and I panic for a moment. I thought she'd use a voice recorder!

But I don't protest. I just try to play it cool while she sets everything up and aims it in my direction.

"Ready. So, Ethan, what have you got for me?" Although her tone has changed slightly now that we have a silent observer recording us, her expression is as disarming as before. As though she's here just for me. Not for the show. Not for Byron. *Me.*

The expectant look in her eyes is enough to make me forget how camera shy I've always been and start talking. I take all the various dishes out of the fridge and introduce them, growing more and more comfortable as I go, until all I have eyes for is her and I don't even notice the lens aimed at me anymore.

She keeps asking me questions about the food, and we even share a bit of banter. It turns into a natural conversation. Just two people bonding over a shared interest. Just like I'd hoped.

And her reaction to the food is enough to make everything worth it. Once she's done tasting a few things I've laid out, it's time for one of the brand new recipes. "Do you like crepes?"

"Do I like crepes? Does anyone *not* like crepes?" she responds with a wide grin on her face.

"Well, sit back and prepare to be blown away, because this is a very special recipe." *Very special.* As in I've not shared it with anyone, not even Byron or the rest of the crew.

"I don't doubt it."

I'm smiling to myself as I start whipping up the batter. This is going better than I'd hoped.

*** Sarah ***

Every single thing Ethan plates up for me is absolutely amazing. From the triple chocolate trifle to the summery lemon and lavender parfait, and of course, the crepes he prepares from scratch right in front of me. But my favorite by far is still that hot chocolate he concocted so effortlessly yesterday and even today. It's as good, if not better than I remember. It's absolutely perfect in its simplicity.

How does he do it?

Although I'm pretty full already, I insist on a refill

after the tasting is over. I take another sip and can't help but lean back in my chair and savor it with my eyes shut. "Seriously. How will I ever go back to a life without this hot chocolate?" I muse.

"You don't have to," he says.

I look up at him and try very hard to keep breathing while our eyes meet. Is he saying what I think he is? "I don't?"

"The recipe is very easy."

My heart sinks again. Apparently not. Even if his eyes are still locked onto mine, helplessly capturing me. Can he not see how he affects me? Or does it just not matter to him?

"I can't even boil eggs without burning them," I try to joke.

I don't feel very humorous right now, though. Dammit, I should just tell him. I should tell him I don't want just the hot chocolate in my life. I want *him*. Well, and the hot chocolate, but only if he's the one making it for me.

I don't say any of that, though. Instead I get through the rest of my questions, and take close-up photographs of all the dishes he's fed me; what's left of them anyway. All the while, I try to find comfort in the fact that I've snagged myself nearly an hour of video footage of him talking about food and cooking for me and looking absolutely dreamy while doing all of it.

I wasn't sure if he'd grant my request of recording him. A part of me was certain he'd be able to intuit that I want the video for myself, to watch in the privacy of my hotel room while imagining *what if.* Like an absolute psycho stalker.

But hey, he works on a TV show, so perhaps he's used to all the cameras by now.

All I know is he's an absolute pro. A natural. If they got rid of Byron tomorrow and had Ethan take over the show, he'd be perfect at it. I'd be his biggest fan. Hell, I already am.

Should I ask him? Should I find out if he has aspirations for his own show one day? He's got what it takes. After working with Byron all this time, he surely must have tons of ideas for his own recipes already. Like that divine hot chocolate.

But I bite my tongue. Because the last thing I want is to make him feel bad. Maybe he likes the way things are? My question would only make things weird between us.

It seems I've run into yet another pitfall of being a journalist: how to balance asking direct and cutting questions while also caring very deeply about what your subject thinks of you. God, it's so much easier writing little articles in the safety of your own office, about people you'll never meet. It's the personal aspect of this assignment that makes it so damn hard.

I guess I still have a lot to learn if I want to be good at this job.

Much too soon, I get through all my questions, without asking anything I *really* want to know.

And I'm so stuffed, I couldn't eat any more sweets even if I wanted to. I'm still no closer to telling him how I feel, and a part of me wonders if that's for the best.

"I guess I'd better get to work on all this." I nod down at my notes.

Ethan smiles briefly. "And I'd better tidy this place up."

"Okay."

"Okay."

We share another look and I force myself into action, disassembling the camera setup and packing everything into my bag.

"I'll see you tomorrow," I say. Ugh, tomorrow. My last full day on set. Time is running out.

"See you." He gives me a little wave.

I exit Ethan's kitchen with a strange heaviness in my chest, as though I'm leaving a part of myself behind. On my way out of the studio, and through the gate to the visitor car parking, I try not to think too much about it. I've had a wonderful time with him. And the food... Oh my God, the food was heavenly. If I hurry to the hotel and get something written up specifically about the food, perhaps I can get Tom to sign off on my new concept before he leaves the office for the day.

And then… Then I'll be able to rush through my article tonight, have it ready for edits tomorrow, and get it submitted with a whole day to spare. And then I can think about what to do about Ethan. But not before I discuss everything with Meg. Hopefully she's free to talk tonight.

I'm in such a hurry by the time I reach my car that I barely notice the dark clouds and onset of rain overhead. Until a few droplets landing on the screen of my phone make reality pretty difficult to ignore. Guess that heat wave is finally over…

I hurriedly dump my bag on the passenger seat to prevent it from getting wet, then rush to the driver's side and notice the flat front tire just as I'm about to open my door.

Dammit!

After whisper-shouting a few curses, I take a deep breath and pull myself together.

So, I've got a punctured tire. It's not the end of the world. I'm a strong, independent woman. I've got a spare wheel and some tools in the back, haven't I? How hard can it be? If I can quickly swap my wheel out, I'll still be on track to call Tom and get my article written up tonight like I planned.

CHAPTER SIX

*** Ethan ***

That went okay, didn't it?

From the way Sarah kept looking at me to all the praises she offered for the sample dishes I'd prepared, it did seem that way to me. And when she said she didn't want to live without the hot chocolate I'd made… She probably didn't mean anything by it, but my heart is still trying to convince me otherwise. Was that a hint? Was I meant to take that as an opening to ask her out?

Part of me wishes I had.

Another part of me thinks I was right to play it safe. Because at least this way I still have hope. I have a beautiful memory of the time we spent, chatting, laughing, sharing our love for good food.

I wonder if I should seek out Claire after I'm done cleaning up, but I decide against it. We could all do with an early night today. So instead, I end up leaving the studio, only to find that the previously hot weather has turned into a grey, soggy mess of a downpour.

Here's the English summer we all know and love.

I wrap myself up tightly in my not-at-all waterproof light jacket and make a run for it to my car. Its trusty engine purrs to life at the first try and I slowly reverse out of my spot right beside Byron's ostentatious new BMW.

Craig, the security guard, doesn't even get out of his cabin when I reach the exit that leads to the public parking lot outside; he simply opens the gate with the press of a button and waves me through.

Sarah was in a rush when she left, so she has to be long gone. Despite that, I'm still keeping an eye out for her. Hopelessly.

Or as it turns out, not hopelessly at all. Among the few parked cars dotted around the otherwise empty lot, I spot her dejected figure standing next to a little red hatchback. She's absolutely soaked. Her wet hair, a few shades darker than normal, sticks to her face and shoulders. Her clothes cling to her feminine figure.

I pull up beside her and roll down the window.

"What happened?"

She abruptly turns around, as if she hadn't noticed me pull up. "Oh, hey, Ethan. I've got a flat."

"Oh dear." I quickly find the umbrella I always keep underneath the passenger seat and unfold it as I get out of my car. I hold it over the both of us—mostly her—while I join her side and inspect the tire. The car is pretty much undrivable.

"I can't get this thing to lift the car up," she complains. "I feel like this shouldn't be *so* difficult."

The frustration in her voice makes me smile, but only briefly. I'm mighty impressed she even tried; I wouldn't have, especially in the rain. "How about I call the AA," I suggest.

"I've got the spare right here. And all this stuff…" She points at the jack and wheel wrench lying on the ground. There's a tremble in her voice when she lowers it to a whisper. "I never signed up for roadside assistance. Didn't think I'd need it."

"It's okay. It's a simple problem to fix." For someone who knows what they're doing. Not me. Or her, evidently. And she should probably get her alignment checked as well before she takes it for a longer drive. It would be best to call in an expert.

She nods and lets out a sigh.

"Why don't I drop you wherever you need to go. Then, I'll get this done for you once the local garage opens in the morning."

She looks up at me with her eyebrows pulled together. "You would do that?"

Of course I would. I would do *anything* for her.

"It's no hassle at all."

*** Sarah ***

That flat tire arrived with excellent or terrible timing. As did the cloudburst signaling the end of the early summer heat wave that had blanketed the south of England for the entirety of this week.

On the one hand, I have mascara running streaks down my face, so I must look like an absolute nightmare. But on the other, Ethan is staring at me in a way I could previously only dream of. Is my shirt see-through? Probably. But he's not focusing on that.

More often than not, he looks away from the road and glances towards me, dripping all over his passenger seat. He does it so many times, I'm grateful that the drive back from Pinewood Studios mostly leads through quiet country roads.

"You don't need the heater on, do you?" he asks.

My knight in shining armor. I suppress a smile and shake my head. "I'm fine."

"If you check the backseat, you'll find a towel—don't worry, it's freshly washed."

Shall I risk it? What the hell; he's offering. And ever since I wasted the opportunity to borrow his jacket yesterday, I've been regretting it. I'll take anything, just as long as it's *his*.

I twist around and try to pick up the folded navy blue towel waiting on the seat behind him, but it's just out of reach. Ethan, however, is closer than ever. He's filling out the driver's seat so well, I'm grazing past his bare arm along the way and it's driving me crazy.

"I can't reach," I grumble.

"I can pull over," he says.

"Just a sec," I say, while undoing my seatbelt and kneeling on the passenger seat so I can fit my upper body through the gap between our seats. I lose my balance in the process, requiring me to steady myself again with one hand on his shoulder.

He's so warm. So inviting. Shivers creep down my spine.

Towel in hand, I pause for a second and just look at him. He's a handsome man, in his own way.

"You have a little—" I remark, only to nearly lose my balance again when Ethan abruptly stops the car at the side of the road.

"What is it?" His voice is low, almost like a whisper, but with a rawness to it which I haven't heard in him before.

"Some flour on your cheek, there," I say, dabbing at his face with the corner of the towel.

He mimics what I've just done and wipes it off with the back of his hand. Then he seeks out my eyes with his again. "Gone?"

I'm lost for words. How close I am to the man I've obsessed about since our first meeting. And I've been trying so hard to keep things professional between us. This is my first solo assignment, after all. The first time Tom has even let me out of the office and into the field. What would he say if he found out I'm dangerously close to seducing the guy I'm supposed to be interviewing? Worse still, I'm actually meant to be interviewing his boss. Instead, here I am drooling over Ethan and spending additional time with him, because I can't stomach the idea of going back and talking to Byron like I'm supposed to.

Objectively I'm failing at my job, but my heart is telling me that I'm on the right track. That this is where the *real* story is.

"Yeah, gone," I whisper.

"Well, we're nearly there," he says, glancing down at my lips for a moment. We are. Nearly exactly where I want to be.

I wish he'd do more than just look. As if he heard that thought, he takes the towel from me and drapes it around my shoulders. His gesture melts my heart and warms my cheeks. If I'm not careful, I'll lose myself in the moment. It would be so easy to follow my instincts and kiss him right now. But what if he's not into it? Or worse still, what if he is, but for the wrong reasons?

I know how I feel; what I want.

If I'm going to do anything like that, I want to make it clear I'm not in this for a one night stand. My heart can't afford to put itself in a vulnerable position like that. If I'm going to give up my credibility as a journalist, I'll only do it for something meaningful.

Something real. But I don't have the courage to follow through on that impulse.

And so I take a deep breath and sit down in my seat again and peer out of the windshield. The clean glass facade of the Premier Inn gleams like a shining beacon up ahead in the first rays of sun trying to break through the clouds. He wasn't wrong. We *are* almost there. Unfortunately.

"Before we call it a night, did you have any more questions for me?" he asks.

It's an excuse; we both know it. After everything we discussed already while he was cooking for me back at the studio, I couldn't possibly have missed anything. But I'm grateful for the opening.

"So many. And I wanted to thank you for helping with my car and the ride back. Why don't you join me for dinner? My treat." I don't know why I say that. I'm not even hungry.

"I couldn't possibly," he says, while keeping his eyes fixated on my lips.

"No?" I breathe.

"It'll be *my* treat."

"We'll see about that when the time comes," I say.

He smiles and slowly raises his hand, bringing it closer to my face. I dare not stir; I don't even dare to breathe until he touches me. His fingertips brush past my forehead and push some errant wet strands of hair behind my ear. Then, his eyes lock onto mine again, and I lose myself.

I can't think. I can hardly breathe.

"May I?" he asks.

"Yes," I whisper, though I don't even know what he's asking me. Does it matter?

Anything he wants. Right at this moment, it's a yes from me. *Anything.*

"I don't know if I'm on the right track here, but I like you, Sarah."

Squeee! I can feel my eyes widen, and my heart speed up, as my cheeks warm and turn an even deeper shade of red. But I just can't move or look away.

"And after the time we spent yesterday evening and earlier... I wonder if perhaps that's something…"

"Yes," I whisper again.

He smiles again and I could just cry. Happy tears, of course. Not that I actually *am* crying; that would be embarrassing.

"This is *so* unprofessional," I blurt out.

He pulls away and leans back in his seat. "You're right, it is."

"No, Ethan!" I place my hand on his knee, and am shocked at how intensely my body reacts to such a simple gesture. My palm is hot and cold all at once. Still, I don't want to let him go.

He turns to me again.

"I like you too. I just wasn't sure—" I stammer.

"You're here on assignment. I understand," he says.

"But knowing that you feel the same, I don't see why we can't make an exception."

"Just this once?" he asks.

The innocence in his eyes makes me smile again.

"Hopefully more than once," I say.

He leans into me again, as I do into him. Our faces meet with just an inch to spare between us. God, he smells so nice, same as yesterday. Sweet, spicy, manly deliciousness. I couldn't tell you if it's an aftershave or not, only that it's the most seductive scent I've ever caught.

It's so heady, in fact, I'm feeling a bit faint now. Or perhaps that's because I've hardly been breathing ever since he pulled over the car. I place my hand on his shoulder to steady myself again. I love how tall he is, even while sitting down. How broad his shoulders are and how much bigger his hands are compared to mine.

These are the kind of hands a man should have. Strong, capable, and warm. But at the same time so very gentle when he touches me. Like he's doing now, placing one of them on the back of my neck as our faces meet the rest of the way and our lips touch for the very first time.

His eyes close, but I force mine to stay open. I

don't want to miss even a second of this. How he kisses me ever so sweetly. So carefully. Like it's this precious thing to be savored. Like he doesn't want the moment to end either, so he's teasing it out as much as he can.

I pull myself into him by his shoulder. His other hand finds its way onto the center of my back. I'm drawn into him; our upper bodies are touching as well now.

Opposites in every way. Big and small. Hot and cold. Masculine and feminine. Only together can we find harmony and perfection.

Too soon, he pulls away and opens his eyes again. I should tell him what I expect. That I'm not inviting him into my hotel room for a casual affair that we'll leave behind as soon as I drive home the day after.

But the tenderness in his gaze tells me we're on the same page. That perhaps, he wants just what I want. *Everything.*

CHAPTER SEVEN

Our first kiss ends much too soon. That's what my heart is trying to tell me, anyway. But at the same time, my other senses are urging me to stop being so bloody selfish.

"You're freezing," I say, as I touch the back of my hand against Sarah's face. Even her lips were cold just now, until I warmed them up with mine.

"It's okay," she whispers.

I shake my head. It's really not.

"Let's go in and get you heated up," I insist.

"Okay." The way she purses her lips and suppresses a smile tips me off to the potential double meaning in my words.

That wasn't my intention, but her reaction stops me from backtracking.

If this beautiful woman invites me up to her room right now for more than just a kiss, I'll be damned if I refuse. This sort of thing just doesn't happen to me. That's more Byron's wheelhouse than mine. The big difference is that he doesn't care about the women he ends up meeting, whereas I've got way too much skin in the game already, and we've only just kissed once. But the door has been opened, and I'm not going to close it without seeing where it might lead.

I force myself to break eye contact with her and put the car into gear. We don't speak another word as we approach the hotel. Not even while I park the car inside the gate near the entrance. All the while, her hand rests on my knee, convincing me that everything is going exactly how it's supposed to.

My fingers seek out hers, interlocking with them as we walk through the lobby and towards the lifts. Like nervous teenagers, we keep stealing glances at each other as we travel up to the third floor, to her room. I don't know for sure what's about to happen, but I know I should pace myself.

She unlocks the door with her keycard and turns on the lights. I'm unsure what to do with myself, so I just stand there, watching with my hands in my pockets.

"You should probably have a shower before you catch a cold," I mumble. "I can wait in the lobby or the restaurant."

"Don't be silly, make yourself comfortable and I'll be right out." She gestures at the pair of armchairs by the windows. So I do.

I sit down and fold my arms. Despite my best efforts, I can't help but track her as she picks out a fresh change of clothes and a clean towel and carries everything into the bathroom.

I'm seriously going to sit here while she strips off and has a shower, just on the other side of that sliding door? As if my mind isn't going to do all sorts of things and go all sorts of places with that mental image? Lord have mercy.

"Get some room service while you wait," she calls out from the bathroom, just before the water turns on.

I exhale sharply and place my hands palms-down onto the armrests of the chair. Room service. Probably a good idea; that way she can relax and keep warm…

Although I immediately pick up the menu from the coffee table in front of me and start to study it, I have no idea what I'm reading. All I can think about is Sarah and our first kiss in the car.

I wish I knew what she's thinking right now. Is she hoping for the same things I am? Or is this just a fling to her? Because I have zero intention of letting her slip away once her time at Pinewood is over. Once we wrap this current season, I'll be free for a few months. Nothing stops me from seeking her out and—

I don't even know where she lives, though.

I know hardly anything about her, except that she seems to love chocolate at least as much as I do. Food can be a shared interest, right? Is it good enough? Could I fit into her life?

The longer I sit there and stew in all these thoughts, the more nervous I get. What even is she doing with me right now? She's beautiful. Young, or at least a few years younger than I am. At the start of a promising career.

And what am I? What have I got to offer a woman like her? I'm just a regular guy who likes to cook. I'm nothing special; nothing much to look at and not particularly successful either. By now I would have liked to have my name on the door of a restaurant and made something of myself. Instead I'm lurking behind the scenes while Byron takes over the nation's cooking scene by storm.

Too introverted to maintain most friendships and too awkward to sweep her off her feet. And that's what she deserves. The full fairytale package. Not me.

The door unlocks behind me, making me snap out of it.

"Hope I didn't take too long," Sarah says.

I turn around and forget myself. Her cheeks are flushed, and her hair—freshly blow dried—is back to its luscious former self. She's a vision that could light up the darkest heart.

"Not at all," I mumble.

"Have you chosen?"

I shake my head. Have I chosen what? As much as my head tried to convince me otherwise just now, my heart chooses her. Something tells me it always will.

That's probably not what she meant.

"I know the menu won't be up to your usual standards, probably. But—"

Right, the room service. "It's fine. I was wondering what you'd like?" I ask.

She smiles. I reciprocate, by reflex.

"Actually, after everything you made for me back at the studio, I'm just too full to eat anything else. You decide." She walks towards me and hands me my towel back. "Thanks for letting me borrow this."

Our fingers brush past each other, and something in me snaps. All my life, I've played it safe. I've always chosen the path of least resistance rather than put my heart on the line. Even this whole thing with Byron; I've always stayed in my comfort zone and put my own ambitions and dreams on the backburner. But right now, with Sarah, I just can't do it anymore. It's time to take a stand.

I take her hand; her fingers thread through mine almost immediately. I try to get up, but she's already on me, straddling me and wrapping her arms around my neck.

This second kiss isn't like the first. Gone is the trepidation we felt back in my car. Gone is the illusion that maybe this is all just a dream; a fantasy that's doomed to play out only once. Her lips against mine give me courage like I've never felt before. For a change, I feel like I'm exactly where I'm supposed to be.

So, I wrap my arms around her and enjoy how she melts into me, surrendering herself to our kiss. But she isn't passive about it. Her arms tighten around me as well. It seems we're both equally desperate to bridge whatever distance still remains between us.

It still surprises me how much smaller she is. I'd mistakenly assumed that meant that she's fragile and needs protecting, but I can feel now that that's not the case. I can feel a surprising amount of strength in her petite frame as she clings to me and I to her.

It makes sense. She's out here trying to live her own dream as a journalist, so she's already many steps ahead of me in that respect. She's courageous in a way that I am not.

And now she's putting all that on the line to share this moment with me?

I can't keep my hands off her, exploring the gentle curve of her back down to her buttocks. Her toned thighs, spread wide across my lap. She fills me with a need I don't recall ever feeling before. A need to please her, to love her and to claim her all at once.

Our kisses intensify, as if we've both been consumed by the same hunger, the same thirst.

I can hardly believe this is happening.

Every part of her perfect body is pressed up into me, threatening to overwhelm my senses and send me over the edge of control. With kisses. With her fingers running through my hair. With hot breaths tickling my face whenever she comes up for air and her shapely buttocks pressing down into my crotch right where it matters.

Are we really going to do this? What if she regrets it? What if I end up disappointing her?

"God, Ethan," she whispers.

Sarah, Sarah, Sarah, my mind chants in response.

"I need to know—" she says.

I force my eyes open and take in the beautiful vision before me. Of her. With her rosy cheeks and slightly moist lips, parted as she tries to catch her breath.

"Anything," I say.

Her hands, resting palms-down on my chest, try to convince me that despite all my flaws, I might just be worthy of her touch. As long as she chooses it. Because she's undeniably in charge of the moment.

Still, it's hard to silence the voice in my head that screams the opposite.

"What I said in the car; I meant it. I'm not after a onetime thing." She pulls her eyebrows together in concern. As if there's any doubt about how I feel. As if I'd treat her as anything less than the queen she is.

"Me neither, Sarah."

"If we're going to do this, you don't get to avoid me and dodge my calls after."

"I don't have your number," I say.

She stares at me for a moment and lets out a most beautiful laugh. "We'd better remedy that first then, yeah?"

"Please."

That's when her phone rings, with uncanny timing. I lean over to pick up her handbag from the other armchair and give it to her.

"I'm not going to—" She takes the phone out and frowns. "Oh!"

"Take it. Don't worry."

"It's my boss." Sarah mouths an apology and gets off me as she raises the phone to her ear.

"Hi, Tom?"

I try not to eavesdrop while I collect my thoughts. Jesus. Now that she's no longer on me, I realize just how close I'd gotten to losing control. My cock is throbbing in my jeans. My skin burns where her hands had just been; such was the intensity with which I'd felt her touch. My heart rate doubled at some point, and I didn't notice until now when it tries to slow down again.

"I'm going to work on a draft tonight. Yes, Tom. Rather than focusing on Byron, I'll write about the food. It'll draw in a wider audience—"

I close my eyes and take a few deep breaths, or try to. Every inch of my skin is buzzing.

It was obvious where things were headed just now. We were staring at the moment of no return together.

If her phone hadn't rung, I might have told her everything she wanted to hear. Clothes would have started to come off.

We would have done things that cannot be reversed or ignored. And she would have etched herself into my heart permanently. Without knowing the truth about me and Byron.

If she *really* meant it, if we're both chasing something deeper than just a fleeting moment together, then how can I justify keeping her in the dark? I couldn't stomach it. She already deserves so much better than me; I can't be a liar as well.

Even though that's exactly what *everyone*—Claire, the crew, Byron, and even the network—expects from me. What they're relying on me to do. It seems I have to pick a side. It's either Sarah or my entire life as it is now. As monumental as this decision is, it's not a difficult one.

"I can make it work, Tom. I'll have something in your inbox by morning. And if you don't like it, I can always rewrite it tomorrow—"

I look up at her, pacing the room. Observing the little furrow in her brow while she listens to whatever is being said on the other end of the line.

"Okay, Tom. I'll get started right away."

The sight of her makes me smile. When she spots me, she stops in her tracks and reciprocates my smile. Yep. It's the easiest choice I've ever made.

"Okay, bye." She hangs up and places the phone on the coffee table. "What are *you* grinning about?"

I shake my head and gesture at her to sit down on the other armchair. She does sit, but on my armrest instead. "Sarah, I have something to tell you."

And just like that, before I get the chance to change my mind, I begin.

"All the food, the entire concept of the show, everything. It's mine. My idea. My work. Not Byron's."

She frowns and opens her mouth to say something, but then just shakes her head and waits for me to carry on. I take her hand and marvel again at how much smaller it is than mine. So much more delicate.

"I told you that Byron and I were working under Jack Cleary at his restaurant in Kingston when he was discovered."

"Yeah." She gently squeezes my hand, as if she doesn't even realize she's doing it.

"That was only part of the story…" What follows is the entire account of how Byron's supposed discovery by the network *really* happened.

How we were indeed working together, but I'd been Jack's sous-chef for a couple of years already, whereas Byron had only just joined the team as a prep chef. How I'd come up with a few new recipes which Jack was trialing at the restaurant. How one day a senior executive from the Home TV Network came in for lunch and ordered one of my new dishes. How I chickened out when the guy wanted to compliment 'the chef' and sent out Byron instead. How that small decision spiraled into a charade that has lasted for almost a year.

"So, in the end, Byron is just there to look good on camera."

Sarah's grip on my hand tightens as she leans in closer. "You look pretty good to me. On camera or otherwise."

I kind of hear what she says, but I don't really believe it.

She rests her other hand on my cheek and kisses me sweetly enough to almost bring a tear to my eye. Funny, how the same act can feel so different every time.

I wrap my arm around her and pull her against me. Our foreheads touch, and I close my eyes and just enjoy the closeness between us. No more secrets.

"Who all knows about this?" she asks.

"It's been an open secret on set, so everyone knows, except the network."

"And you've never wanted it for yourself?"

I just shrug and smile. "I'm not cut out for the spotlight. Byron might be a terrible chef, but he's so much better at all this other stuff. I'm just content my recipes are finding a wider audience."

She lets out a chuckle. "I thought it was just me not knowing how these shows are shot normally, but yeah. I guess he *is* pretty terrible, isn't he?"

I don't reply; I just sit there with my arm still around her.

"You're lucky I like you," she whispers. "Or you should have never told me any of this."

"Yes I am. The luckiest."

And that's why I can't stay. I won't let things play out like they were about to just now, before that phone call. That's not the kind of guy I am.

CHAPTER EIGHT

*** Sarah ***

Ethan left ten minutes ago, and my thoughts are still all over the place. If not for Tom's ill-timed phone call, tonight would have gone in an entirely different direction. But instead of falling into bed together, we connected on a much deeper level.

Before our interruption, I'd wanted to make sure we were on the same page. That it wouldn't just be a onetime thing ending in disappointment. Rather than placate me with potentially empty promises, he put himself on the line.

He shared his biggest secret.

It was the one thing he should have *never* shared with any outsider, especially not a reporter. The one thing that could destroy Byron, the show, and everything he and the rest of the crew had worked for.

And once he did that, he suggested we pick things up tomorrow, over dinner. Like a proper gentleman. I'm weak in the knees even now, just thinking about it.

Tomorrow evening, my article will be done and

my time at Pinewood almost over. I'll have nothing else to think about except the two of us and where we're headed.

We'll go on a *real* date, not whatever this was turning into.

And although my body is reeling from all the sensations and desires our make-out session inspired in me, I can't stop grinning. That means we *are* on the same page. He's not just trying to get in my pants. Because despite the interruption, that's exactly how tonight would have ended. Our chemistry is too intense and my willpower too weak.

If he's willing to take his time, that means he's as invested as I am. And that's why he told me everything. It's all so much to digest.

Byron Ainsworth is a fake.

I'm not even surprised, really, because he seemed pretty damn fake in every way already. What shocks me more is that Ethan let it happen, even orchestrated the entire thing from the start. For what? So he can get shouted at on set? So he has to lie to anyone who comes along, maybe even himself?

The crew, of course, know better, because Byron so obviously hasn't got the required talent or skills in the kitchen. I should have realized it as well after watching the first day of shooting. The only reason I didn't was because I've had my head on backwards ever since meeting Ethan… Beautiful, kind, compassionate, and oh-so-very-sexy-without-realizing-it Ethan.

But now I know. And I don't know what to do with it all.

Unfortunately, I still have work to do. No matter how much I want to just spend the entire night reliving my time with Ethan and imagining a happy dirty ending for the both of us, I'd promised Tom a draft by morning. A write-up almost entirely about the food, so I can get our readers excited about the upcoming season and avoid lying all at the same time.

By the time I left Ethan's kitchen earlier tonight, I had entire sections of it already forming in my head. All I have to do is put them down onto the page. Despite all that, most of that inspiration is long lost once my laptop boots up. So, I start downloading the footage of Ethan cooking for me, and make myself a mug of instant coffee. Then, caffeinated drink in hand, I settle down on the bed again with the laptop balancing on my thighs.

My heart starts to race while I go through all the videos of him.

'Byron is just there to look good on camera,' Ethan had said.

Bullshit. Byron-effing-Ainsworth can't compare to what I'm looking at right now. Am I really so biased that I'm seeing things nobody else would? The way he's moving around the kitchen, plating up ingredients with a level of effortless confidence that Byron couldn't muster in a million years? There are no dozen-or-so takes. There are no do-overs. Ethan cracks a few eggs into a bowl, adds some flour, milk, and whatever else and cooks up perfect crepes for me without batting an eye.

I pull up YouTube in a separate browser window and start looking through snippets from the previous season of *Decadent Desserts*. The production is slick. Every episode looks polished and professional, but the editing is quick and at times misleading.

I start to imagine all the stuff viewers don't get to see. All the hours of rejected footage left behind in post-production. All the curses and frustration and the numerous takes they have to go through for Byron to look halfway decent at whatever he's doing.

I take note of the subtle differences between the dishes he's preparing and the close-ups at the end which look so much better. Because Ethan prepared those in his kitchen. Far away from all the cameras.

The production crew has done an amazing job. They've fooled me as well as the rest of the nation into believing that Byron is everything he's pretending to be. When they always knew better.

But they had a job to do: to create a great cooking show. One that would draw in new viewers to the Home TV Network. And they've excelled at it.

No wonder Claire was unhappy when I showed up

yesterday. Because my presence was a threat to everything they'd worked for. Nobody wants to get cancelled.

I sigh deeply and open a blank document. A big gulp of coffee later, I close my eyes and let my fingers loose on the keyboard. I free-write my first draft, recapturing those first impressions of the food. How seductive it was. The flavors, aromas, textures… How the whole experience made me feel. How I imagined being fed these things in a much more intimate setting. How food can be foreplay, if it's made right.

Or, if it's made by the right man… I don't name any names for this last part. Everyone will think I mean Byron, but I know my truth.

Ethan is the real star of the show, as I've learned tonight. No matter what the cameras have captured and Claire and her team have packaged and sold to the viewers.

Ethan is the real deal.

I keep going back to my footage of him and analyze absolutely every facet of our interactions. How things start off a bit awkward, but he loosens up while talking about the dishes he's chosen. The reserved excitement in his voice. How his back straightens just a little every time I compliment the food just off-camera. The hint of a smile playing on his lips while he anticipates my reaction to every next thing he introduces me to.

And he thinks he's no good at this and doesn't want to be the center of attention. I call bullshit.

I can't pretend to know Ethan very well yet, but I think I know enough to come to a very big conclusion by the time my first draft is done.

He secretly *does* want it. He wants the recognition. He wants the credit.

Maybe he never imagined having his own TV show, and so the thought will take some getting used to. But if he had no real ambition, why join the kitchen of a Michelin starred restaurant? I've seen a couple of interviews of Jack Cleary in the past and he doesn't seem like an easy boss to work for. If he didn't have a drive to succeed, then why not pick an easier, less stressful job?

If Ethan went so far as to pitch new recipes to Cleary during his time there and actually got them on the menu, he must have had certain dreams for himself. Maybe he wanted to go out on his own one day and have his own restaurant. Maybe a whole chain of them. Maybe he dreams of having a cookbook out with his name on the cover, topping the bestseller charts nationwide.

Whatever it is, I'm sure Ethan never planned to stay in the shadows forever.

Why else would he tell me? I'm a reporter, for God's sake. It's literally my job to expose truths. But the last thing I want is to betray his confidence.

Ugh!

I read over my article, and make a few tweaks here and there. Although it's decent and fits the brief pretty well, I'm not happy with it. Because it only furthers the charade.

I write a quick note to Tom before reluctantly attaching my article, when my phone rings yet again.

This time it's Megan. *Finally!*

"Hey! It's about time you called me back!" I tell her.

"Girl, what do I tell you. Tom is killing me with deadlines."

"Psht, you've never had a deadline you didn't beat."

"That may be so, but I've never had a life outside work before either, and Dean and I are getting pretty serious," she says.

I smile. "How long has it been now?"

"Almost three months."

"I'm so happy for you!" I really am. Any jealousy I might have felt earlier has faded, thanks to what's been developing between Ethan and me.

I lean back against the pillows and can't stop smiling. "I actually have a little bit of news of my own."

"Say it ain't so!" Megan exclaims.

"What?"

"You had your one-on-one interview with Byron

and he swept you off your feet just in time for you to turn in that article to Tom. And your initial hatred of him has turned into a torrid enemies-to-lovers style affair."

"Oh, please!" I make a face.

"Then?"

"Well, there's another guy who works on set. Another chef." *The chef*, in fact. My whole body seems to float whenever I think of him. Talk about him.

"Tell me more," Megan demands.

"Well, he's amazing," I say, then bite my bottom lip. In order to explain just how amazing he is, I'd have to share his secret. With another reporter. Can I risk it?

"Oookay…"

"What I'm about to say next, you can never repeat to another living soul," I warn her.

"You're killing me. Just tell me already."

"He's…" I close my eyes and mentally go through all my memories and impressions of Ethan. "I'm going to send you a video, okay?"

"Sure."

"Right." With the click of a few buttons, I pull up a fresh email window and attach the video of Ethan preparing crepes for me. "Just let me know what you think."

"It's not here yet," Megan complains.

"It's a big video and the wifi here sucks."

"Well then, keep talking to me in the meantime!"

"It all started when I arrived on set the other day. I had just introduced myself to Byron Ainsworth, in his dressing room—" I say.

"You were in Byron-flipping-Ainsworth's dressing room?!"

"Stop! That's not—" I take a deep breath. "I'm just having a quick chat with him, and realizing what a terrible slime ball he is. And in walks the most incredible guy—"

"I think I've got the email now," Megan says.

"It was amazing. I was awestruck."

"I know what that's like."

"Literally, it took me like two seconds to figure out: I need to see more of this guy while I'm here," I say.

"So, what did you do?"

"I made sure I could interview him, of course!" The hot chocolate incident comes to mind and makes me grin like an idiot.

"Of course! Was there much talking, during this supposed interview?" she asks.

"You're too much!" I complain.

"I'm not the one banging my subjects."

"I didn't—"

"Relax, girl. I'm only teasing you." I can hear Megan chuckling on the other end. "And I've got that video, hang on."

"Okay."

She goes quiet for a while and I have my heart in my throat. What if she doesn't like Ethan? What if I am just that biased and I'm seeing things that aren't there? Then again, what do I care if she likes him or not; is that going to change my opinion of him? I would think not.

"Jesus, he's tall, isn't he?" Megan says.

"He is."

"Almost as tall as Dean."

I make a face at the phone. Of course, she's making it about Dean again.

"You recorded this yourself? It was just the two of you?" Megan asks.

"Yeah, why?"

"Just. The way he's looking at you… Like *you're* dessert."

I hit 'play' on the laptop and watch it again myself. He *is* looking at me a lot, isn't he?

"He's done for. You've got him. Hook, line, and sinker," Megan says.

I can't help but smile. I knew that already, of course. Considering what he told me before leaving tonight. But it's nice to get confirmation from an impartial judge.

"He dropped me off at the hotel tonight," I say.

"Oh! Then how come you're on the phone with *me* right now?"

"Well, it was the most incredible thing. Things were going really well, we were about to, *you know*… And then Tom calls."

"Fucking Tom," Megan scoffs. "Always getting in the way."

"Right. But it made us stop and think, you know? And then Ethan told me something. Something he should have never told anyone. Said he didn't feel right keeping secrets from me. And we're going on a proper date tomorrow night."

"Don't tease me, woman! What did he tell you?"

"He told me in confidence…"

"Sarah Walker, if you don't tell me right now, I will hunt you down and force it out of you! Violently!"

"He told me…" I take a deep breath to try and overcome my nerves. "He told me Byron is a fraud. The recipes, the entire show, it's all basically *his*. He just didn't want to be on camera."

"Holy shit balls!"

"And now I'm stuck, you know? I've written my article for Tom, sort of. But knowing what I know now…"

"You love him?" Megan asks.

"Isn't it a bit too soon—"

"Don't argue with me and don't over-think. Do. You. Love. Him?"

I close my eyes again. I know the answer, it's just

hard to say it out loud. "Yes," I whisper.

"What does your heart tell you to do?" she asks.

"I don't want to betray his trust. But I also want to help him realize his dreams. And I think deep down, maybe he does want the recognition. And despite what he said, he's incredible on camera. You saw the video."

"I'd watch this every day of the week," Megan confirms. "He seems much more personable than Byron. Like you're at a friend's house for a dinner party, watching them cook. Like he's enjoying every second of it."

I let out a sigh of relief.

"Well then, you've got a big decision to make, don't you? On the one hand you have the article you were *supposed* to write. On the other, you want to help what's-his-name's career, but you're not sure if he really wants that for himself."

"*Ethan*. His name is Ethan." And the more I think about it, the more certain I get that he *does* want it. Call it intuition.

"Right, Ethan. So you'd better get off the phone right now and work it out before you miss Tom's deadline, yeah?"

"Yeah." I press my lips together. "Thanks, Megan."

"Any time, girl."

As the line goes quiet, I check the time. Eight-thirty. That leaves me with less than twelve hours to figure all this out. Before I get the chance to second-guess myself, I pick up my phone again and make another call.

"Sorry to call so late, Claire. But I need your perspective on something—"

CHAPTER NINE

*** Ethan ***

Last night went so much better than I could have imagined. I'm still on cloud nine when I turn up at the studio bright and early in the morning, and that feeling carries on for the rest of the day. Even Byron's complaints aren't enough to put a damper on my spirits. Nor is the fact that I barely slept all night, because I kept running through everything that happened in Sarah's hotel room. Again and again. Like a man obsessed.

I still don't know what she's doing with *me* of all people, but does it matter?

The first thing I do is to call the local garage, to get her car fixed. It fills me with pride to be able to do this for her. Take care of her. I wish I could spend the rest of my life doing just that…

Only then do I dive into my own work.

I've only got to get through the rest of the day before we're alone again. Tonight, I'll make sure to do things properly. I'll wine and dine her and make a real effort to get to know her as a person. I'll pamper her like the queen she is. And then…

RECIPE FOR PASSION

It'll be her last night in town. I have to make it count. Although she already knows a bit about how I feel about her, I have to make it clear just how serious I am. I think she's the one. And she deserves to know it. Plus, there are logistical issues to think about. I'll be stuck here while we shoot the current season, but after that, I'd follow her across the world if she'll let me.

I know what her lips feel like against mine. What she tastes like. What her body feels like in my embrace. What her hair smells like, freshly out of the shower.

I know that she's the woman I've been waiting for my whole life.

I still don't even know where she lives, though, because I never got the chance to ask. Tonight, I'll lead with that. Before we inevitably get distracted by our chemistry, which appears to be mutually intense.

The hours pass slowly while I work on today's recipes. I haven't seen Sarah all day, so when I finally emerge from my kitchen after shooting finishes, her presence is a sight for sore eyes.

"Hey, Sarah!" I wave at her from across the studio, where everyone is running around tidying up their gear for the day. More than a few heads turn, first in my direction, then hers.

She smiles sheepishly as we approach each other.

"Here," I say, handing her back her car keys.

Her eyes brighten immediately. "Aw, you got it fixed?"

"I said I would." I put my hands in my pockets and just stare at her. It's the only thing I can do to stop myself from taking her into my arms and kissing her in full view of the entire crew. And although I wouldn't really care if everyone saw us, I don't know how she would feel about that.

"That's amazing. Thank you!" She grins.

That smile. That smile could kill me.

"This is going to sound crazy, but—" I take a deep breath. "I couldn't stop thinking about you all day." And night. Oh lord, the long, sleepless night I spent fantasizing about her. But I don't say that.

She averts her gaze and stares at the ground while her cheeks turn a few shades pinker. "Same."

That's good, right? I want to tell her how I *really* feel. I want so badly to tell her I love her. Because I think I do. I'm pretty sure I do. But something is holding me back. I'm probably making her uncomfortable. She doesn't seem as free as every other time we spoke. My mind goes into troubleshooting mode.

"Did you finish your article in time? How did it go?" I ask. My question makes her look up at me again, but she isn't smiling anymore. It seems that I've honed in on the problem.

"Yeah… It went."

"Was your boss—Tom, right?—not happy with it?" I ask.

"No, no, he's—just a few more I's to dot and T's to cross, that's all."

"Let's talk in here." I gesture at the door leading to my kitchen.

"Okay."

Once inside, she seems to relax, but only slightly, and I can't let it go.

"Is something wrong?" I ask. "If there's anything I can do to help…"

She smiles bleakly, but doesn't immediately speak.

"Ethan, what you told me last night—"

"Yeah." I sit down on one of the chairs lining the wall, but she doesn't join me straightaway.

"It's been bothering me ever since," she says.

"I'm sorry."

She shakes her head and finally does sit down on the chair next to me. "Don't be. *I'm* sorry."

Why is she apologizing to me? I frown and shake my head. She still looks unhappy and I don't know what to do about it. Do I take her hand? Do I try to comfort her?

She takes a deep breath and straightens her back. "Are you really fine with the way things are with Byron? With the show?"

I shrug. "Look, it is what it is now. It's not a bad deal."

"What if you could go back and have whatever you wanted? Would you choose to play second fiddle again? Or would you want what's due to you?"

I shake my head and frown. She's disappointed in me, isn't she? She thinks I've made the wrong choice here.

"If I could have *whatever* I wanted, I'd be fifty pounds lighter, a lot more sociable, and I suppose yeah, maybe I'd want some recognition for what I do here." I fold my arms across my chest and try to breathe. But the frustration is only growing and it's about to strangle me.

She's disappointed in me. Bloody hell. That's why she looks unhappy. Can I blame her? I'm no catch.

"The thing is, you *can* have whatever you want," Sarah says.

Can I? I shake my head again and study her pretty face. I thought I knew exactly how today was going to go. And what I wanted most of all was her love and respect. I wanted a chance at a life together and I thought honesty would get me there. Instead...

And just as it did last night—with the worst possible timing—her phone rings.

I don't even say anything.

"Fucking Tom!" she grumbles, then answers the call while mouthing an apology at me. "Hello?"

I can't make out what's being said on the other end, but Sarah's face falls even further. "Are you sure? I'd like to avoid that if possible."

She chews on her bottom lip as she listens to Tom's response.

"Well, I suppose he's going to find out once it goes live, anyway. You're right. I can't keep on pretending. I'm no good at it anyway."

Find out what? Is she talking about me?

And how has she been pretending?

"Okay, I'll hold you to that. More than just one round of drinks, though!" She presses her lips together, then her eyes settle on me again.

'I can't keep on pretending.'

Even now as she hangs up the phone and fully focuses her attention on me again, I can see the change in her. Within the span of ten minutes or so, everything has changed.

Pretending. This one word keeps echoing in my brain until I can't think straight anymore.

Of course she was only pretending. All those little moments I thought we shared? She's a hell of an actress. She had a job to do—to get a cracking story—and so she did everything she could to earn my trust and make me reveal things I shouldn't have. And like a sucker, I fell for it all. I was the weakest link.

"Ethan, I'm so sorry to cut our conversation short, but I've got a few changes to make to my article before Tom leaves for the day. Those T's and I's I was talking about earlier. We'll talk properly over dinner later, okay?" she says.

Dinner? What's even the point of carrying on this charade?

None of this should have surprised me, and yet it feels like the spot where my heart used to be is just a gaping cavern. To say I'm crushed doesn't quite describe how I feel.

So, this is what it's like. Betrayal. Heartache.

What an idiot I am.

"Give me about half an hour? I'll meet you back here, or in the parking lot?" Sarah asks. "And do you know where I might find Byron right now?"

Byron. For all his arrogance, he does know women a lot better than I do. He would have never let this happen. He would have never let anyone get this close. With my rose tinted glasses on, I was too blind to see the obvious.

Everything Sarah did, everything she said to me, it was all a means to an end.

Because of my naivety, she's figured out that Byron is a fake and she's going to expose him. The show will get cancelled. Bye-bye, future plans. All these people we work with every day will have to look for other jobs. Byron—well, fuck Byron to be honest. He never deserved the spotlight anyway. But Claire and the others? They did the best with what they were given. It's not their fault. It's mine.

"Half an hour? Ethan?" she repeats herself.

My chest grows tighter, and I instinctively ball my fists. I want to scream, just to get a handle on all these emotions, but I take a deep breath instead.

Focus, asshole! For once in your life, don't be a fucking coward. Say what needs to be said. Do what needs to be done!

"Actually, you know what? I'm good," I say.

"Huh?" I try not to look at the confused little frown that's making half a dozen cute little crinkles appear on her forehead.

Stop it, you idiot! Stop looking at her!

"It's almost the end of your time here in Pinewood, anyway. You should get some rest tonight and I have plenty of work to do as well. Let's not waste each other's time any more than necessary."

"But, I thought—" She doesn't complete the sentence. And I don't give her a chance to.

"Really. It's okay," I say. It's not okay. A part of me wonders if anything will ever be okay again. I get up and grab my bag. "Bye, Sarah."

"Okay… Bye?"

I avoid the sight of her as I quickly leave my kitchen, and she doesn't say anything else to stop me either. As the door slowly closes between us, I feel like I'm leaving my heart behind and it *hurts*.

That's it, then. Reality has reared its ugly head and the fantasy is over. It was always too good to be true, right from the start.

I should probably give Claire fair warning about what's about to happen. She's always been kind to me. And I just ruined her show. I'm not looking forward to this conversation.

CHAPTER TEN

I used to think I would do anything it takes to get a good story. *Anything.*

My experience this week already taught me that that's not the case. Because I can't leave my feelings at the door. I can't sell out.

Something Tom told me when I first got this job is still rattling around in my head. *'At one point or other, you have to decide: what kind of journalist do you want to be?'*

I thought I knew what I was doing. I'd made my choice and had a plan. I wanted to maintain my credibility. I wanted to write about something—someone—I truly believed in.

I didn't want to use this assignment to protect the status quo, but to make a positive change. To give Ethan the chance to claim what was always rightfully his. And get a damn good story out of it too.

It's a real scoop, as Tom called it. And I had everyone on board, except Ethan himself. As usual, I got ahead of myself and messed everything up. I thought he was different. Everything seemed to be going so well. We were going to go out on a proper date, even!

Over the course of one conversation, sweet, kind-hearted Ethan turned into , a complete douchebag. *Waste each other's time?* Was that what he was doing? Has he been toying with me? What about the special hot chocolate? The whole episode when he rescued me out in the rain yesterday and drove me back to my hotel? Making out in my room and setting a dinner date for tonight… Was it all just a game to him?

I don't fucking believe it!

Shock makes way for anger.

He pivoted pretty damn quickly when he overheard that we were going to publish the truth. As if that was always his end game. How dare he! He's lucky I already submitted my article and I've got too much riding on it to take it back, or else… I let out a deep sigh and my entire body deflates as my heart caves in on itself.

Tears are clawing their way out of the corner of my eyes and there's nothing I can possibly do to stop them.

Why did this have to happen? I steered clear of Byron, because I got serious douchebag vibes from him. But Ethan too? They're both cut from the same stinking cloth.

I can't believe I thought he was the one. I can't believe I poured my heart out into that article. To top it all off, my feature is going to launch his career. The same feature for which Tom and the marketing team have been building buzz all week. He's even upgraded the article and commissioned a video, using snippets of Ethan cooking for me. The network will be all over him to take over the show and *I* will have made it happen. *Me.*

I finally force myself up when I realize I'm running out of time to get the final piece of the puzzle Tom asked for. Byron's reaction. The crowning glory to this cluster fuck of a day.

And it had started off so promising! I even managed to get Claire on my side, which was most surprising…

I tighten my grip around the car keys in my hand and start walking. *Whatever.* Let's get this shit over with. Even if Byron screams and shouts at me when I tell him, he couldn't possibly make me feel any worse than I already do. I'm invincible in my misery.

With renewed purpose and rage fueling my progress, I reach Byron's dressing room. I raise my hand to knock on the door, only to have it open in my face. That same make-up girl I'd seen on my first day on set is leaving in a great hurry, and only narrowly avoids colliding with me.

"Sorry. Are you okay?" I ask.

She doesn't make eye contact with me, just nods quickly and makes her escape. Was she crying?

I'm still frowning, when Byron's complaints from inside the dressing room distract me. "At least clean up after yourself, you useless cow!"

What an asshole.

"Can I quote you on that?" I ask, pushing my way through the door. "Maybe give me some context as well, though."

Byron raises his arms in a defensive gesture when he realizes who he's talking to. "Sarah. Lovely to see you! It's just… The girl has left a mess over here. She does this all the time."

"Uh-huh." I glance at the single used cotton ball left behind on the otherwise spotless dressing table. I suppose it's never occurred to him that if only he were a bit more pleasant with her, maybe she wouldn't be so flustered that she'd forget to pick up after herself before leaving.

I take my recorder out of my bag and hold it up in between us.

"I wasn't aware we had another interview scheduled today," Byron says.

"We didn't, actually."

"Right. Because I'm quite busy."

"Not for long," I grumble.

"Excuse me?" Byron snaps.

Sure, I'm being unnecessarily abrasive. But since I'm already mightily pissed at how things went down with Ethan, I'm ready to burn my bridges on the way out of this place. I can't believe I'd ever turn into this, but right now I'm channeling my inner Piers Morgan. I'm not sure I like it. And neither does Byron.

"Byron, I was hoping to get your reaction to some news we've just learned."

"Oh yeah? What news?"

"That you're not actually the brains behind this show. That all this time you've been pretending to be someone you're not."

He's still frowning when he opens his mouth in protest. But he doesn't speak. Then he takes a step back and sits down and takes a deep breath.

"Okay. Who told you that?" he asks.

"I have my sources."

"Still. It was Claire, wasn't it? She's hated my guts since day one."

I purse my lips and stare him down. Maybe I should just tell him it was Ethan. Get his unfiltered reaction to his betrayal as well. I can't quite bring myself to, at least not yet.

"Is there anything you'd like to tell your fans, now that the truth has finally come out?" I ask.

"I…" Byron shakes his head and stares at the far side of the room behind me, then he lets out a soft chuckle. "Look. What would you have done?"

I raise an eyebrow. Not be an insufferable prick, for one.

"Someone hands you a golden opportunity like

that. Wouldn't you take it?"

I suppose, maybe. But that's hardly the point. "You took someone else's recipes and pretended they were your own. What do you think your fans would say about that?"

"I didn't *take* anything. I was *given* recipes. I was playing a role, like an actor."

If you put it like that, it almost sounds benign. I wonder what Ethan would say about that. But then again, screw both of them.

"I've always wanted to be an actor, you know? But everyone knows how hard it is to get into show business. So, I did the sensible thing. I learned a trade." Byron smiles briefly. "I got into culinary school. It wasn't my first choice, but it was supposed to be a way to earn an honest living."

My hand is trembling a little bit now that the adrenaline is starting to wear off.

"So, it *was* just an act," I say.

"I thought it would be good fun, you know?" Byron sighs. "A way to get everything I'd dreamed of, while skipping the hard part. Auditions. Acting lessons. All that stuff. Thanks to the magic of television, it all just sort of fell into place."

I nod. The magic of television, indeed. A casual observer would never have noticed everything I observed last night when I rewatched clips from the last season. Because unlike other TV chefs, Byron doesn't do live appearances. No morning talk shows or daytime television. Nobody from the media had ever been allowed on set before either. It was all carefully set up so he wouldn't be found out. Until I came along… No wonder Claire was so annoyed the day I arrived.

"I can tell you, not having to ever try and temper chocolate again in front of those spotlights and cameras… that's kind of a relief."

His admission makes me frown again. Today is turning out very differently from how I thought it would.

Ethan isn't the man I thought he was. And neither is Byron. Did I get *anything* right during my time here? At least the food is still the food, right? And I'm still a reporter. Sort of. If only I can bring myself to ask the right questions, finally, and leave my heart at the door.

"So, your reaction to being found out is… relief?" I ask.

Byron makes a face. "I kind of wish it wouldn't have happened this soon… But… I feel like I've had this hanging over my head since day one. I just thought that as long as I played the part of a star, maybe I could fake it until I made it, so to speak… In a way it's easier now that it's over."

I sigh deeply and shake my head. "Okay. Well. Thanks for your comments."

"Yeah…"

I switch off the recorder and just stare at him for a while. He doesn't really look like the same guy anymore either. Like all the pretend has melted away, and maybe he really is an actor. One who can finally take off his mask.

"What are you going to do now?" I ask him.

He shrugs. "Good question. I guess I can always change my name, move to another country, and try to get a job in a restaurant kitchen again…"

Something tells me that's not going to happen.

"As long as you don't ever have to temper chocolate again," I remark.

He smiles briefly. "Yeah, I'd like to avoid that at all costs."

Well, that was bizarre. Byron looks to be in his own little world when I leave him behind in his dressing room. I almost feel for him, but then I remember how much of a dick he's been to everyone around him, and my sympathy circles back to… myself.

Yep. Now that I've vented my frustration at Byron, all that remains is self-pity. But this is no time to wallow. I still have a little work to do.

CHAPTER ELEVEN

*** Ethan ***

I'm gutted when I finally locate Claire, who is just getting ready to leave, much earlier than she normally would.

"Got a minute?" I ask in a choked voice.

She stops packing her scruffy old shoulder bag and looks me up and down once. "Ethan. I was hoping to catch you on my way out."

"Oh, right?"

"You go first," she says, chewing mindlessly on her bottom lip with a thoughtful frown on her face.

Suddenly, I have no idea what to say or how to start. I take a deep breath and say the only three words that come to mind. "I fucked up."

"This is about Sarah?" Claire asks.

I run my hand through my hair and shake my head. "No, it's totally my fault. I mean…"

"Having second thoughts, are we? Don't back out on me now! I've already talked to the network and they've been looking for a reason to make a change anyway. Apparently some anonymous complaints have been made against Byron. The only reason we didn't pull the plug before today's shoot was because the lawyers needed to go through Byron's contract first and we didn't want to tip him off."

"Once that article goes viral—hang on… *What?*" I stare at her for a moment, wondering whether her words mean what I think they do.

Claire smiles bleakly at me. "It was always going to come out, you realize. I thought we might at least get the current season out of it before shit hit the fan, but… Eh." She shrugs. "Plus, once the story breaks, it'll create massive buzz for the new show, so that's something."

"What kind of change is the network looking to make, exactly?" I stammer.

"You. Taking over. Sarah called me last night to put out some feelers before sending me her article."

"She told you? Jesus, why am I only hearing about this now?" I ask.

"I figured you two would have discussed this over… Dinner. Or whatever you were doing last night when this whole thing came about." Claire tries to keep a straight face, but I can clearly see the flutter in the corner of her mouth. "In any case, I'm happy for you both. You make a pretty cute couple."

Words evade me and all I can do is stand there and slowly shake my head.

"You've read it, right?" she asks.

"Read *what?*"

Claire leans down and starts rummaging in her bag before handing me an unassuming print-out. "Here. It's really rather sweet. You've made quite the impression."

As soon as my eyes scan the first few lines of text, my heart starts to race uncontrollably and it feels like the ground falls out from under me. Oh, shit!

"Jesus," I mutter.

"Hey, what are you doing here with me, anyway?" Claire asks. "I would have thought you'd want to spend more time together, seeing as she's leaving tomorrow."

I look up at her, then back down at Sarah's article, then at the large digital clock on the far side of the studio. We *were* planning to spend the evening together, before I opened my big mouth and ruined everything. And with the way I left things with Sarah just now, I shouldn't be surprised if she never forgives me. For what, a stupid conversation I overheard? That could have been about anything! But I just had to make it about myself and my dumb insecurities, didn't I? I had to take the one perfect thing that's happened to me in my entire life, and stomp all over it before it could lead anywhere.

I groan. "I'm such an idiot."

"Relax. I'm sure she'll forgive you even if you make her wait a little," Claire says.

I can't breathe. I can't think. I have to go.

"Congratulations on getting your own show, Ethan! We'll set up a meeting with the network in the morning!" Claire calls out behind me. I don't even look back.

Shit. She wasn't pretending about a damn thing last night. I realize I'm still holding on to the copy of the article Claire gave me, and I start reading it again. This isn't a cold-hearted expose; this is as close to a public declaration of love anyone could hope for. She poured her heart out onto the page.

And what did I do? I insulted her and blew her off.

It's going to take a lot more than some hot chocolate to fix this. So, what the hell do I do? Chocolates? Flowers? Teddy bears? No. I can't bribe her into forgiving me.

All I know is I'd give *anything* in the world to be able to make this right.

* Sarah *

The short drive to the hotel and trip up to my room pass in a blur. As does the process of writing up my brief single-paragraph account of Byron's reaction to the news, which I immediately forward to Tom. Job done just in time, before I completely fall apart.

Soon after, I find myself in the bathtub, downing half a bottle of wine ordered from room service.

Neither the hot water nor the alcohol do anything to soothe my aching heart.

I thought Ethan and I were at the beginning of something beautiful. Obviously, I was wrong. I was wrong about a lot of things this week.

A part of me wants a shoulder to cry on, but I just can't pick up the phone. My pride prevents it.

My thoughts circle back to him and every time they do, the tears return, until my head is pounding and I hardly have the energy to cry anymore. Even the water has turned chilly by now, and I can't be bothered to top it up anymore.

So, I force myself onto my feet and wrap a towel around my shoulders. That only reminds me of last night in the car, when Ethan did the exact same thing. And I choke on my own emotions yet again.

Snap out of it, woman! I tell myself.

This is ridiculous. No matter what I've been trying to tell myself, I barely even know Ethan. We only met for the first time a couple of days ago! Why should this hurt so much?

No matter how hard I try to reason my way out of this mess, my heart disagrees. That same heart has been making plans and imagining a future with him. And as such, I didn't just miss out on what would have been a romantic dinner date tonight; I lost the chance at something a lot more significant. But that would warrant feeling disappointed. Not *this* .

For as long as I can remember, I've always trusted my instincts to help me make the big decisions in life. When I switched to journalism halfway through college, I did it because it *felt* right. That's also how I decided to join *Celeb Roundup* after graduating, when everyone else in my life was telling me to apply for local newspapers instead. To become a *serious* journalist. But no, I had to do it *my* way, because my heart said so.

And this thing with Ethan was the same. My heart said yes, so I dove in headfirst.

Never before has my intuition let me down this badly. If I can't rely on that to make halfway decent decisions in life, then what do I have left?

Nothing. That's what.

And *that's* why I'm hurting so much. As soon as I realize this, I just let it wash over me again. No big deal, I'm just having an existential crisis. Maybe one day I'll look back on this moment and take it as a learning experience. *Maybe*—

There's a knock on my door, which makes me flinch. Room service, again?

"Just a moment!" I dump the towel on the chair, then hurriedly put on a robe and secure it tightly with the belt around my waist.

As soon as I unlock the door, I freeze. It's not room service at all.

"Sarah, I'm sorry," Ethan says. "Shit, you've been

crying."

I don't even know what to say, so I just stand there with my mouth half-open and stare at him in disbelief for a couple of seconds.

"What are *you* doing here?" I say, finally. "I thought you weren't going to waste any more time with me."

"I…" Ethan looks up at the ceiling, then down at the floor, and everything in between. Just not directly *at* me. "I've come to apologize. Grovel. Beg. Whatever it takes."

Again, I'm speechless. And now my heart is racing. I fold my arms in front of my chest, then unfold them again.

"I didn't know, Sarah! I thought—" He cocks his head to the side and glances at me with a pained expression on his face.

As crushed as I still feel, I can see he's in bad shape too. And for some reason, I still care.

At least hear him out, the little voice in my head says. *You'll regret it forever if you don't.*

Will I? Or will he sucker me back in, only to let me down later on, when I'll regret not slamming the door in his face? I just don't know anymore.

"When I heard you on the phone with your boss, I misinterpreted everything. I thought that it was all too good to be true. That you were only pretending," he says.

I shake my head in disbelief. "Pretending how?"

"You said that you couldn't keep on pretending. Naturally, I assumed—"

"You thought that was about *you and me*? Why would you even go there?"

"Before the call, you looked so uncomfortable. Like you didn't really want to be around me," he says.

I close my eyes and groan under my breath. Could it be that this entire mess was just a big misunderstanding?

"I was terrified, because you told me something in confidence, and I went behind your back and wrote it up anyway. I didn't know how you'd react," I mumble.

"Claire showed me the article."

A couple passes Ethan in the corridor, shooting cautious glances in our direction, prolonging the awkward silence between us. I suddenly feel very exposed standing here in just a robe with the door wide open.

"Come in," I tell him.

As soon as the door closes behind him, I take a deep breath—in and out—and at least *some* of the tension leaves my body. My knees are still trembling, though.

"Sarah, I…" Ethan starts, then just stands there with his hands buried deep in his pockets.

Then it dawns on me what he said just before I

invited him in. And my nerves surge yet again. "You read the article."

"I did."

Well, what did you think?

He sighs and shakes his head, then he straightens himself, as if he's really forcing himself to confront me. As a result, my heart starts to pound, and I brace myself for what he's about to say. My conversation with Byron turned out to be mostly a non-event, but now I'm thinking that *this* will become the grand finale of today's shit fest.

"The whole day—no, since last night, actually— I've been thinking about how I wanted tonight to go. Needless to say, things turned out very differently."

"Right." I can only manage a whisper.

"I left the studio over an hour ago, came straight here, and sat parked in that same spot where we pulled over last night, thinking about what to say to you. I made notes, even, so I wouldn't forget anything." He lets out a sad chuckle and sighs.

Here it comes. He's about to tell me how betrayed he feels because I exposed his secret. How it all went to shit because I messed up. I catch myself clenching my jaw and try to force myself to relax. It's impossible.

"You know what I wanted to do tonight? I wanted to have a nice meal together. Get to know you better. And maybe by the time they'd serve dessert, I'd take your hand, and…" He takes a deep breath. "I wanted to tell you that from the moment I first saw you in Byron's dressing room, I knew. I knew that you were the one. I probably would have chickened out, because I don't deserve you, but that's what I *wanted* to tell you."

My mind goes blank. I blink a few times and stumble a couple of steps backwards before I'm able to catch myself against the backrest of one of the armchairs. This can't be right, so I just end up shaking my head.

"Sarah. I've never felt like this before. For God's sake, I don't even remember the last time I asked anyone out. And even though I read your article multiple times, I still can't believe it. I can't believe how close I came to getting everything I could ever want, with a woman, who's just—you're amazing. And I'm—"

"But I betrayed your trust." My head is spinning.

"When you were asking if I was really okay with Byron being in the spotlight, I thought you were disappointed in me. That you regretted what happened between us."

"I wasn't—" I stammer. "Everything you told me last night; I couldn't put it out of my mind. And I thought that deep down, you were unhappy with how things were; that's why you opened up to me. If I could just tell the truth, everything would fall into place—"

"You were trying to help. I see that now," Ethan says.

"I shouldn't have gone behind your back."

"I shouldn't have jumped to conclusions," he says.

"I'm sorry, Ethan!"

"No, I am." He takes a step in my direction and runs the back of his hand down my cheek. "I'm so sorry I ever doubted you."

Our eyes meet, and time seems to stand still. There's so much to see. How torn up he is about everything. There isn't a doubt in my mind that he means every word he's just said to me. Maybe my instincts haven't betrayed me after all.

I feel my body deflate yet again, but this time it isn't in defeat, but rather in relief.

"Ethan. If you're not onboard with all of this, I can fix it. I can retract the article—"

He smiles briefly and shakes his head. "Claire made it abundantly clear it's too late for second thoughts."

"Oh."

He cups his hands around my face and just keeps on looking down into my eyes.

"Sarah."

"Yes?"

"How did you know?"

I pull my eyebrows together.

"How did you know I did want it?"

His question snaps something inside my chest and tears start to flow again. So, this is what redemption feels like.

"Don't cry, baby, please," he whispers.

I put my arms around his neck and melt into him. By the time he reciprocates and embraces me tightly, I'm a sobbing mess. I want to tell him I'm not sad anymore. That I just need to relieve the tension that's been accumulating ever since I left Pinewood. But the words evade me. So, in the safety of his arms, with my face pressed into his warm chest, I just let it wash over me.

He's here now. Neither of us have anywhere else to be. We'll talk when I'm able.

CHAPTER TWELVE

*** Ethan ***

When I arrived at the Premier Inn and knocked on Sarah's door, I didn't have much of a plan. I only had a pocket full of notes which I'd prepared in the car. My own declarations of love for her, which admittedly were much less eloquent than what she'd put in her article.

I'd considered *everything* before I got here. At one point, I almost drove off to find a jewelry shop to buy her something meaningful. A ring. Or a pendant. Anything.

But that didn't seem right either. I settled on having to rely on just honestly telling her how I feel to sort out this mess. Considering that she's in my arms right now, I suppose I made the right choice.

I do wish she'd stop sobbing though, because I'm pretty close to losing it as well. And nobody needs to see a big thirty-four-year-old man ugly cry, especially not the girl he's been trying so desperately to impress.

"I'm sorry," I whisper, while caressing her damp hair. Over and over again, like it's somehow going to make everything alright.

Countless minutes pass before she stirs and pulls away from me. Her face is wet and her eyes red and puffy. It's hard to look at her like this, but despite everything she's still the most beautiful woman I've ever seen.

"You look so tense," she remarks. The sweetest little smile breaks through her previously serious expression when she places her hand on the side of my face.

"I never meant to make you cry," I say in a choked voice.

"These were happy tears. Relieved tears. Something like that."

I exhale sharply, but the tension in my chest has barely reduced. "Okay, then."

She takes my hand and threads her fingers through mine. I'm overcome with so many feelings, and I don't know what to do with any of them. This is where it all started last night. When I forced myself to do something— *anything*—just to grasp the moment instead of letting it slip away.

I remember everything she's written. Everything she's intending to publish. I've never been much of a ladies' man. I never thought I was capable of inspiring such feelings in anyone, never mind in a woman as stupendously out of my league as she is.

You've made quite the impression, Claire had told me. That was an understatement.

RECIPE FOR PASSION

I saw it written in black and white, in Sarah's own words. How her world changed after we met. How she instantly knew that Byron was nothing special, but *I* was. How my cooking seduced her, because she could see I was doing what I loved and genuinely wanted to share it with her. How those moments together made her feel…

She'd instinctively caught on to what I was trying to do: win her over with food. I just never imagined it would actually work, because really, who the hell am I?

Just an awkward overweight chef, who might cook a seven course meal without batting an eye, but has no clue what to do when faced with the woman of his dreams. And yet here she is, looking up at me with those big expectant eyes of hers, convincing me to just follow my instincts, and…

I let go of her hand and cup her face again, guide it towards me before leaning down and kissing her. The softness of her lips breaks my heart. The tickle of her breath against my face chokes me up and finally brings a tear to my eye as well.

The way she's stretching her arms around my shoulders as far as they'll go makes me wish I wasn't such a great big freak, just so our bodies would be more compatible. She's so small compared to me; how is this even going to work?

But there's no hesitation in her touch, as if she's

oblivious to all these truths. She runs her hands down my back like she owns me, which to be fair, she does. She's had me right from the moment of our first meeting.

My body reacts viscerally to her affections, as does my heart. Like a caged animal, which has finally caught a first whiff of its mate, I'm overcome with urges and desires too crude to put into words. I want to break free from the confines of right and wrong.

Just like last night, she doesn't seem to mind when I put my big, clumsy paws on her. I can no longer stop myself. My hands reach the curve of her hips, just as she tightens her grip on me and lifts herself into my arms. I'm much too happy to help her along. Anything, just to get even closer.

Her robe opens below the belt, revealing the naked flesh of her thighs, as she tries, but fails to wrap her legs around my waist. I hold onto her bare skin to keep her in place, and my mind goes blank. This is it. The point of no return.

Our lips never part for more than a breathless second as I stumble towards the bed.

I try to lay her down gently, but it goes slightly wrong when she refuses to let me go and I lose my balance and end up on top of her. Any passing concern I might have had about hurting her is wiped away by the feverish kisses she continues to unleash on me.

She's so small, but she doesn't seem fragile anymore. She's in control of the moment, whereas I'm just a helpless passenger.

Now that she no longer has to lift herself up from my shoulders, her hands start to explore my body through my clothes. My back, my sides, my ass. I feel so inadequate compared to her, and yet… She tries to kiss my doubts away one by one.

It's too much. My hard cock presses uncomfortably into her thigh. I raise myself onto my elbows and look down at her beautiful face. I can't believe she's letting me get this close.

"Sarah," I stammer.

"Ethan, don't stop." She grabs the back of my neck and guides me back down for further kisses.

I can't resist. Even the awkwardness of realizing how my thick body is crushing into her isn't enough to discourage me. I do exactly as she asks. I don't stop kissing her. I don't stop touching her. I run my hand across her naked thigh, and upward underneath the dressing gown until I force myself to pause on the side of her hip. Am I going too far?

The pressure is building to uncontrollable levels. If I carry on grinding into her thigh like this, I'm going to—

"Ethan," she mumbles. "Ethan, take your clothes off."

It's such a simple demand, and yet it kind of isn't.

"Are you sure?" I ask. It sounds like such a dumb question now that I've said it out loud.

"Hell yes, I'm sure. I need you!" she whines.

Shit, if you put it like that.

I take a deep breath and pull my t-shirt up and over my head.

She bites her lip and grins at me as she runs her fingers through the curly hair in the center of my chest. Although I still feel out of place, I don't ever want her to stop. I need her touch like a plant needs water.

"Very nice! Now show me the rest," she demands.

Her eyes lock onto mine when she reaches down and tugs at the belt of her gown. The robe slips off her shoulders and more of her naked body comes into view. God, I'm so inadequate. So undeserving.

Perky breasts, flawless skin, slender waist. Everything about her is perfection. She could be a model, whereas I'm…

"My God, you're gorgeous," I mumble.

"So are you," she whispers.

I glance down at the juxtaposition of our bodies. There's so much I would change, just to be worthy of this moment with her.

She follows my example and also gazes down at where our bodies meet. At all the excess where a flat, toned stomach should have been. How it rests heavily against the gentle curve of her lower abdomen.

RECIPE FOR PASSION

I expect her to retreat. Or at least to acknowledge how fucking weird this is. How mismatched we are. How criminal it is for someone like me to—

"Ethan, make me yours," she says instead. Her voice is raw and full of need. She grabs a handful of love handle and looks up into my eyes again. "Please, baby. I want you."

And that's enough to get my head, as well as my body back in the game. My cock stiffens up once more. I raise myself just enough to unbutton my jeans with one hand. She eagerly takes over and starts pushing them down off my hips along with my boxers. My erection springs forward, as if it knows exactly where to find salvation. She spreads her legs as wide as they'll go and guides me in.

My mind goes blank as I do anything and everything I can to slow down. This is the second time we've been building up to this moment. At the very least I should perform.

With my eyes tightly shut, and my breath held, I try to figure out a rhythm that works for both of us. Slowly, deeply, gently. All the while my body is screaming at me to speed up. I'm so close, I can almost taste it. I'd never forgive myself if I let this moment pass too quickly.

Her body is gripping me tightly, as if she won't ever let me go. I can't believe she wants this as much as I do. Why me? Why not someone more worthy?

Someone as beautiful as her?

Then I open my eyes again and I see her looking up at me. With her dark hair fanned out across the pillow and her full lips gently parted, she's a vision to behold. An angel. A queen. A goddess.

"Fuck, that feels so good," she moans.

I can only answer in grunts, not words, as I carry on making love to her. Slowly. Deliberately.

"Ethan, you turn me on so much!"

Beautiful angel. You have no idea what you're saying.

And yet… Every time I move, in and out, I feel an overwhelming sense of power. Of purpose. Then, I wonder if she's imagining someone else. Someone better. But when I look down, I find her still staring at me. And just to wipe the last shred of doubt from my mind, she begins to whimper my name every time our bodies join. That's when I finally start to believe. I'm exactly where I'm supposed to be. Doing what I'm meant to be doing. Her wish is my command.

My hips are moving with a mind of their own now. My attention is fully on her pretty face. Running my fingers through her hair, down the side of her cheek, tracing the delicate curvature of her lips.

"Sarah, Sarah, Sarah," I whisper. Or maybe I just think it. I don't know.

She smiles at me, and my heart rejoices. We're doing the unthinkable, and yet she's happy. *I'm* making her happy.

All the while, her hands are on me. Touching me all over without a hint of trepidation. Like she knows exactly what she wants and... it's me.

"I don't know how long—" I grunt.

"Stop talking. Keep going," she says.

She takes my hand and places it on her breast. *Oh fuck.* I run my thumb across her nipple and she wiggles against the mattress and makes the most delicious little noises.

I do exactly as she asks; I do keep on going. And with every thrust of my hips, I'm getting inevitably closer to the edge. Until I'm staring down at the gaping abyss where I know pleasure resides. I can't stop it anymore. I can't put off the inevitable.

"Yes. Harder," she moans.

My mind goes numb, as instinct takes over fully and I give her everything I have left. She bucks her hips into me and cries out my name.

"Oh, god. Ethan!"

I can feel her body clenching up. She grips me tightly, inside and out, and I finally lose myself as my cock unloads inside of her. Shivers pass down my spine as I tremble and shudder into her, desperate to keep moving, and yet completely incapable of it.

She digs her fingers into my ass and just keeps me stuck in place, deeply buried inside of her.

It's intense. Insane. Impossibly beautiful.

I'm fighting just to stay propped up on my elbows,

but she keeps clawing at my back until I surrender and settle down on top of her. I try and fail to catch my breath as she runs her hands through my hair and down my shoulders and back.

"I'm sorry," I whisper.

"For?"

"I didn't want to finish so quickly," I say, while kissing the side of her face, and rolling onto my back next to her. With her arms still tightly wrapped around me, she ends up on top.

"I couldn't have lasted longer even if I tried. Plus, we can always do it again. And again." She dives down for a long, slow kiss, and I know she's right.

We *will* do this again. As long as she carries on wanting it. Wanting *me*.

CHAPTER THIRTEEN

How much can change in an hour. From having the worst day, I've gone to being on top of the world. Or, being on top of Ethan. In my case, that's the same thing.

My damp hair sticks to his bare chest as well as my own face, but I don't let it bother me. I don't try to think about how I must look, sans make-up and puffy-eyed. I didn't even have the chance to put on any perfume or even deodorant before he arrived.

He certainly doesn't seem to care. His arm is protectively wrapped around my shoulders, keeping me in place with my head resting in the center of his chest.

This. This is where I want to be for the rest of my life. Here I have everything I could ever want.

Ethan's breaths finally start to slow, though mine haven't quite yet. I'm still overcome with a sense of post-orgasmic bliss I've never felt before. A sense of temporary calm, because I'm fully aware I'm in the eye of the storm and it could sweep me up again at any moment.

And I can't stop caressing him. I love his hairy chest. I love how warm and soft he is all over. How broad his shoulders are. How I fit into his arms. How I can literally lie on top of him and it doesn't seem to bother him at all. And how he absolutely dominated me when he was on top of me earlier. God, that was magic.

"I love this." I sigh, while tracing the light brown fur around his right nipple with my fingertip. "You're like a big sexy teddy bear."

"Oh yeah? What else do you love?" he asks.

"Umm, everything about you."

"Not possible," he says.

"You calling me a liar?" I poke him in the side with my finger and he twitches. Then, he tightens his arm around me again.

"Why me?" he asks instead.

I look down at him. At the concerned frown that forms on his face while he tries to make eye contact with me. He looks so disarmed right now, it's making me want to confess all sorts of truths.

"This is going to seem sudden," I say. "But last night, after you left, I had a realization. Or rather, I had a talk with a friend, who forced me to have a realization."

"Oh?"

"I told her *everything*. About you, what happened last night, including what you told me. I asked for her advice and she countered with a question—" I take a deep breath. Say it! Now or never! "She asked me if I love you."

Ethan raises his eyebrows, but doesn't say a word.

"And I said…" My throat narrows, causing me to whisper the rest. "I said yes."

A tremor passes across his face, like a series of micro expressions I can't quite place. But he doesn't let me go, instead holding me even tighter. I realize he's holding his breath, and so am I.

"I… Sarah, I love you too."

I don't even let him finish before I kiss him again. It's all I can do to relieve the tension of the moment. Once I feel like I can think again, I pull back and rest my hand flat on his chest. God, he's so sexy. And so adorable all at the same time. Does he have any idea how he affects me?

"Have I done the right thing with the article? Talking to Claire?" I ask.

He sighs and smiles briefly. "Honestly? I'm terrified."

I take his hand and hold it tightly. "The world deserves to see how talented you are. To see everything I see."

"I'm just a regular guy. I don't know how to—"

I shake my head. "Wait a second."

Although it almost hurts to leave the safety of his arms, I force myself up anyway. Ethan also sits up, resting his back against the headboard while I grab my laptop and place it beside us on the mattress.

The video I'd taken of him is already open when I wake the laptop.

"Everything you need to know is right here," I say, hitting play.

He looks uncomfortable watching himself at first, so I crawl back into his arms and start giving a running commentary of everything I've observed during the hundreds of times I've replayed this clip. How confident he looks. How capable. And at the same time, how friendly and personable. Because he's doing what he loves. He's the polar opposite of Byron, who just seems grumpy and miserable when he cooks on camera. Because he's really no good at it and knows it.

Then, I pull up the clips of the actual show to illustrate my points.

Ethan doesn't say much. He just keeps holding me and caressing my hair.

"You were already doing all the work coming up with recipes and making the food behind the scenes. What's his contribution? Nothing, except a bad attitude," I conclude.

"How'd he take it?" he finally asks.

"Byron? Like he knew it was coming," I say.

Ethan chuckles softly. "That's what Claire said. That it was inevitable. Apparently, the network has received some complaints against him, even."

That makes me feel a bit better. Perhaps I wasn't meddling after all; I was just giving fate a helping hand.

Before I get the chance to say or do anything else, he shuts the laptop, takes my hand, and pulls me into his lap, facing him. As he kisses me, again and again, I realize that this is it now. My new favorite place. Until we change position and I discover yet another one.

It's all perfect, as long as it's with him.

"Hey," he mumbles, while pulling back just far enough to look into my eyes. "Where do you live, actually?"

His question turns me serious again. Funny. I've never asked him this either.

"Milton Keynes," I say.

"Oh, thank god. I was worried it'd be somewhere far, like Scotland or something." He smiles and pulls me into his embrace again.

"You?" I ask.

"Kingston."

Of course. That's where he said he and Byron worked before getting signed for the show.

"That's not too bad," I remark.

"No, it's not."

"We can easily meet each other after work. And on the weekends…" All the time, basically, until he's sick of seeing my face.

"We might even go on a real dinner date one of these days," he says.

I chuckle. "I'd like that. One day. What are you doing tomorrow night?"

"Why, are you busy right now?" he asks.

"I already have plans." I take his hand and put it on my hip, before grinding down into him. He's ready. As am I. Ready to see where tonight will lead us, and ready to enter the next phase of our relationship.

I never understood how Megan decided in one night together that Dean and she were meant to be. But now I do. Because that's how I feel about Ethan. From the moment I saw him, I knew it. I knew that he was special, and that I needed him in my life. And although I've done my best to sabotage things, by going behind his back and trying to fix things that I didn't even know for sure were broken, I stumbled into perfection. The perfect relationship for me. With the perfect man.

Tonight is only the beginning. As it turns out, my intuition wasn't wrong after all. It led me to this moment right here with him.

I just have to show him how I feel. I just have to reach out and keep loving him, safe in the knowledge that he loves me too.

Everything else will work itself out eventually.

EPILOGUE

One Year Later.

Time flies when you're with the man of your dreams. Ethan and I have been an item for a year, and we couldn't be happier. He's in the midst of shooting the second season of his very own show, and I'm joining him on set like I usually do when I have some time off work.

We're back at Pinewood, inside building TV One, where our story started.

The studio might be most famous for producing many a James Bond movie, and hosting more TV shows than I could ever hope to name. But for me, none of that matters. This will always be the spot where Ethan and I first met, and as such it holds a special place in my heart.

Although the main building still looks like it did back then, they revamped the actual set as part of the rebrand ordered by the network prior to Ethan's takeover. There's an audience section now, and the seats are fully booked as usual. We can hear the murmur of the crowd through the door of what is now Ethan's dressing room.

It's almost time for him to go on. The make-up girl starts to pack up her things and leaves us, so we have a much-needed moment alone.

Ethan is still sitting down in front of the mirror, and has begun organizing the index cards he has prepared to remind him of all the recipes he is going to do today. I remember how he told me he'd prepared notes to talk to me that night when he came to my hotel room. When we finally became a couple. That memory makes me smile all over again.

I approach him from behind and rest my hands on his shoulders. He's so tall, even though he's sitting down. I love it. I love everything about him.

"Nervous?" I ask, though I already know the answer. I even love that about him. He's so very humble; he still doesn't fully believe that there's a whole audience out there, just waiting to watch him do what he does.

"It's not going to get any easier." He looks up at me and smiles briefly, then goes back to studying his notes for today's episode.

Ironically, adding the live audience was Ethan's idea. He said having a few people there who'd actually taste the food would make it seem more like a restaurant setting. Just the prospect of feeling all those eyes on me would have made me even more nervous, but not him. He needs the personal connection. To see the excitement in their eyes.

And from 'a few people', the setup grew pretty quickly as his show started to gather followers. Today, there's a few hundred.

"You're going to be amazing as usual," I tell him.

"You're just saying that because you have to," he counters.

I lean over and wrap my arms around him from behind. "Are you calling me a liar?" I whisper, nibbling on his earlobe.

He shifts back in his seat and rests the side of his head against mine. "I love you."

"I love you too."

A knock on the door interrupts, and one of the new interns peeps inside. "You're up in two."

"Thanks, Eve," Ethan says.

I love that he makes it a point to know everyone's name, everyone's story. That even though he's the star now, he still goes out for drinks with the crew at least once a week. Because they're a team, as he says. And without them, he would be nowhere, because there would be no show.

Ethan straightens his back and I reluctantly let him go.

"Your adoring fans are waiting for you," I say.

He chuckles. "Here today, gone tomorrow. The only adoring fan I need is right here in this room."

He knows just what to say to make me smile. As

he gets up, I notice that he seems a bit more stiff and tense than normal. Is he planning to do a particularly complex recipe today?

I catch up with him just before he reaches the door and place my hand on the side of his neck. We share a quick kiss in the doorway.

"You'll do great. Go, break a leg," I whisper into his lips, just before we're forced to let each other go.

He only smiles briefly and nods.

Once outside, applause erupts as Ethan makes his way onto the stage. I, meanwhile, rush to my seat in the front row. The intro music plays and Ethan starts to talk, welcoming his audience to his kitchen.

Although he looks a little bit more comfortable now that he's on stage, I still can't shake the feeling that there's something off about today. It's putting me on edge. I catch myself gripping the armrests of my chair so hard, my knuckles are turning white.

"The first recipe I have for you today is so easy, anyone can make it, and yet so delicious, you'll never need another one. But before we get into that, I wanted to share a little story with you all..."

My eyes are glued to him. I'm mesmerized, just like I was in what was his prep kitchen at the time, in this very building, watching him closely while he cooked up the most amazing cup of hot chocolate. Funny, how it's been a whole year already, and yet I remember that moment like it was yesterday.

"…Hot chocolate," Ethan says.

My ears perk up. Did he actually just say that or did I imagine it?

"And so, one year exactly to the day, I feel like the time is right…"

"No way," I mutter under my breath.

Ethan makes eye contact with me from the stage, smiles briefly, and puts his right hand in his pocket, before walking down the steps and stopping right in front of me. There are about half a dozen cameras and spotlights trained on the two of us at this moment. I can't breathe nor think, so I just stare at him like a deer caught in headlights.

"Sarah Walker. You're the best thing that's ever happened to me. And I know you could do a million times better than me, but for some strange reason you've chosen to spend the past year with me. I can't imagine my life without you in it. Everything I have is thanks to you."

I press my lips together and try not to fall apart while literally everyone in the building is gawking at us.

Ethan pulls a little box out of his pocket, gets down on one knee, and holds it up in my direction. "I know I don't deserve you, but I was hoping that *maybe, just maybe,* you'd want—"

Oh god. That look in his eyes. I literally have to choke back the tears.

"Sarah, will you be my wife?"

That's it. I've come undone. Tears are streaming down my face as I get up out of my seat and stumble across the last couple of feet separating us. I wrap my arms around his head and shoulders, which still come to about chest height despite him kneeling down. God, I love how tall he is. Just as I love everything else about him.

"Yes, yes of course," I sob.

He surrenders to my embrace and I all but wrap my entire upper body around him, kissing his hair, the side of his face, just anywhere and everywhere within reach.

We're still clinging onto each other, when I notice the roaring applause that's erupted all around. I look up, partially blinded by the spotlights, and I see all the faces looking at us.

Nearly the entire audience is weeping right along with us, applauding wildly and chanting our names.

Although it's pretty intimidating to be in the center of attention, I get it now. I finally understand why Ethan insisted on the audience rather than just a few cameras. These are his people. His tribe. He doesn't just go on and cook a few things, cash his check from the network, and leave again. He's made an actual connection with every single one of them, by sharing his love for food in a way that only he could do.

That's exactly how he tried to connect with me,

exactly one year ago today. Great food is his love language. And that's a powerful thing.

He gets up in front of me and takes my hand. I watch breathlessly as he slides the gorgeous Victorian style diamond-and-sapphire-studded ring onto my finger and places his hand on my cheek.

"I promise I'll always love you, Sarah."

I sniffle back further tears and press my lips together to try and get my emotions in check.

"Me too. Always," I whisper.

A new chant has swept across the crowd. The excitement is palpable in the air, and impossible to ignore.

"Kiss the girl! Kiss the girl!" they shout in unison.

"May I?" Ethan asks me, cupping my face in his hands, like he always does. As if I could ever refuse.

"Always," I say.

He leans down, just as I raise myself onto my tiptoes and tighten my arms around his neck. Our lips meet, and the resulting roar from the audience matches perfectly the torrent of emotions boiling over in my chest. He sets my heart alight just like the very first time. And in this moment, I know this is how it's going to be forever.

I will love him as intensely—as passionately as I do right now—for the rest of my life. And he will love me right back.

Fame and fortune might come and go, as he always makes sure to remind me. But together, we have everything we need right here. In each other's arms.

AUTHOR'S NOTE

Thanks so much for reading *Recipe for Passion*.

Perhaps you've been following me for a while, perhaps you're new to my work. But now that you're here, I'd like to give you a little background on how this book came to be...

My writing career started all the way back in October 2012 when I took a very deep breath, closed my eyes, crossed my fingers and even my toes and clicked 'Publish' on my first short story. That steamy little piece called *Ladies' Day*, and the book it grew into eventually ([Beautiful Stranger](#)) are still relevant today because it features a curvy heroine and her older lover. It serves as my first foray into steamy body positive romance.

Since then, I've published a whole bunch of other books, in various romance sub genres; as L. Moone I write contemporary, and as Lorelei Moone I write about shifters, vampires and other paranormals. Certain themes tend to repeat themselves throughout my catalogue.

Beauty lies in the eye of the beholder. The hang-ups we tend to have about ourselves and our bodies often aren't shared by the opposite sex. While it's a lot more popular to write about gorgeous curvy ladies and their athletic admirers than the other way around, but I've dabbled in both in the past. I just never felt there was a big market for husky men in romance. 2020 changed that thanks to the likes of Jessa Kane and her sexy big boy titles, *Hefty* and *Husky* (she published a few more similar titles by now). I'm slowly seeing other authors enter this space, so perhaps the time has come? I hope so, because I'd love to write a whole bunch more of these...

Love at first sight is another theme I write about quite a lot, both in my paranormal books as well as the contemporary ones. In fact, I have an entire series called Chance Encounters that follows three couples who casually hook up, only to find that they don't really want to say goodbye after. What they recognized as lust, turned out to be something a lot more intimate.

If I had to pick a third, then it would be messed up characters. Perfection is boring to me because if you put two flawless people together there's no conflict; no drama! Some of my characters have physical flaws, while others might be a bit neurotic or otherwise eccentric. That's what keeps things interesting for me as a writer. I hope you, the reader, feel the same.

Anyway, this book signals the start of a new era for me as a writer. A chance for me to reconnect with my roots of writing inclusive romance about people (yes, men also) with different body types. Just because someone doesn't look like an underwear model, doesn't mean they can't have a scorching happily ever after with their soul mate. And this book is also a continuation of sorts, a promise that my brand is and forever will include: *Happy Endings for Underdogs*. If you enjoyed this book, and can't wait for the next installment in the *Husky Men Do It Better* series to come out, I do hope you'll check out some of my other husky men books while you wait: Just Another Day at the Office and One Night Stand.

And that's enough from me. I hope you enjoyed the story as much as I did while writing it, and if you're interested in reading more of my work, perhaps you'll consider signing up for my newsletter. I'll even give you a free short story when you sign up.

x, Lorelei

YOUR NEXT READ?

Recipe for Passion isn't the only big boy romance book I've written over the years.

It's actually the start of a new series, called Big Boys Do It Better, which is going to release throughout 2021.

But until then, do check out the following titles:

Bloody typical. Day one at the new job, and I'm crushing so hard on my colleague I can't think straight.

John isn't your average romance novel hero. He doesn't have a way with the ladies, neither does he have six pack abs. He's just a regular guy with a bit of a dad bod, and he's shy and awkward rather than suave and charming.

That's cool, because I'm just a regular girl. One who's already head over heels for him and he doesn't even realize it...

Available to order from all major book retailers - ISBN: 9781913930028

I was only looking for Mr. Right Now…

All I want is a night of distractions to take my mind off the stressful business meetings I've had day. At the pub, I quickly spot the perfect counterpart to share tonight with. Whereas I'm all business, he's tall, burly, long-haired as well as tattooed. We're nothing alike, and yet click almost immediately.

Could it be that I have accidentally stumbled across Mr. Right?
Available to order from all major book retailers - ISBN: 9781913930080